T0156587

THE PRINCE

AND THE

POTTER

BY SAMEER GROVER

FOREWORD BY REV. TRUONG THACH DHAMMO

iUniverse, Inc.
New York   Bloomington

The Prince and the Potter

iUniverse books may be ordered through booksellers or by contacting:

*iUniverse
1663 Liberty Drive
Bloomington, IN 47403
www.iuniverse.com
1-800-Authors (1-800-288-4677)*

*ISBN: 978-1-4401-2402-0 (pbk)
ISBN: 978-1-4401-2404-4 (ebk)*

Printed in the United States of America

iUniverse rev. date: 2/27/2009

For my parents and my brother

FOREWORD

I have known Sameer Grover for almost seven years now. Over this time we have developed a really close friendship. Sameer is a generous and compassionate man who is an inspiration to many, he has taught me a great deal about both life and the English language. He is an avid practitioner of meditation and enjoys spending time in nature. I am the abbot of Khmer Kampuchea Krom Buddhist Temple, and I have fond memories of taking many walks with him around our temple and the surrounding community. Sameer and I have given several lectures together on Buddhism, and his words are as eloquent in person as they appear in this book. His calm presence has had a profound influence on me and is something I will always remember him by.

Ananda's story begins by paralleling the life of Buddha Gautama. A unique twist occurs when Ananda leaves the princely life to learn the Buddha's dharma, which was recently established. In this section of the story, the author presents the teachings of the Buddha. Even though the Buddha's teachings are over 2500 years old, they are now more pertinent than ever. *The Prince and the Potter* is a concise but essential piece of literature that conveys the true insight of the dharma. This is the first work in the promising literary career of Sameer Grover, and I eagerly anticipate the future works of my dear friend.

Rev. Truong Thach Dhammo
Stoney Creek, Ontario
December 2008

CHAPTER 1

The morning sun peeked through the treetops, smiling upon the riverbank below. A multitude of hues of crimson, pink, violet, and orange glistened off of the sacred river. High above, in the vast and open sky, far above the shadows of trees and forest, above river and land alike, an elegant white swan gracefully made its passage towards the sun. The swan rose on the limitless air, flew an invisible course, a path without a trace. Its journey was one that would inspire all those that witnessed this phenomenon to spread their own wings and to soar.

The young prince Ananda sat alongside his servant and companion, best friend and confidante, Keshava. They sat beneath Ananda's favourite banyan tree on the riverbank, just off the shore, at the edge of the palace grounds. They often sat beneath the shelter of this majestic tree and observed the arising and passing of the waves of the sacred river. Keshava attentively observed Ananda who was engaged, as usual, in thoughtful reverie. A gentle breeze blew through the prince's wavy mane of black hair. His eyes were piercing and dreamlike, penetrating and blissful.

"Every wave that arises will come to pass," Ananda said. "It is only a matter of time before each rising wave falls and returns to the river to form new waves; these new waves will then rise, reach their crest and fall, returning to the river to form ever new waves once more. Each individual wave in the river is impermanent. Transience is the law that governs the fleeting lives of the waves in the river."

The golden sun bathed the rich brown skin of both young men in the warmth of its resplendent rays. It bathed them in the same way that it bathed the river and the land, the rabbit and the fox, the sunflower and the daffodil. Keshava admired the young prince for his equanimity and unconditional love. Although Keshava was of the *shudra* caste, the serving class, Ananda always treated him as his perfect equal. Ever since they were young they had been the best of friends, despite the caste distinctions that would have broken the bonds of a lesser friendship.

Ananda's gaze fell on the opposite riverbank. On the other side of the rushing river, a lush forest grew freely at the base of a towering mountain. The majestic mountain, adorned in dense foliage, sloped skyward with its lofty peak dwelling high above the clouds forming a palace in the sky.

"I know what you are thinking," Keshava said. "Even this mighty mountain, this haughty symbol of fortitude, it too will come to pass in time. The day will come when this mass of rock and granite comes crashing down and crumbling to its knees. The life of this mountain is also rooted in impermanence, as are those of the towering banyan trees. They, too, will one day fall to the ground and return to the earth from whence they came. The same thing can be said of the brilliant sun in the sky. This beautiful sun will not shine forever. The time will come when this sun, when it too, ceases to rise and set. The same holds true for the moon and the stars, the clouds and the earth, and even the river. This sacred river, most holy of all beings, will not flow incessantly. It too will dry up and cease to flow. It is only a matter of time."

"Yes, we are all inextricably bound to the laws of time," Ananda replied. "The lives of all of the people that we know, every last one of them, are also rooted in impermanence. The nobles and the servants, the dancers and the entertainers, and even the Brahmin priests who perform animal sacrifices and chant holy mantras, their lives are all transient. Even you and I, Keshava and Ananda, our lives are also subject to the laws of time."

Ananda was full of sorrow and compassion for the all too fleeting and fragile existence of the myriad forms of life. How could one find lasting peace, find any solace, during their brief sojourn here on Earth if the ocean of impermanence was simply going to wash it all away in time? Although Ananda scarcely knew or realized it, he had encountered the foremost dilemma that plagued all great philosophers, poets, and sages during their lives at one time or another. How could one find rest and inner peace in the midst of a constant state of transience? How could one find lasting happiness when everything around them was always changing?

The young men left the riverbank and walked in silence for some time. Ananda decided then and there to resolve the questions of his heart. They parted ways as Keshava went to the servants' quarters, and Ananda approached the palace. Upon reaching the entrance, Ananda paused to gaze at the majestic white marble and stone building that basked in the sun's glow, casting shadows upon the flower garden that lay before it. Ever since he was a boy, this majestic structure- where his family and several other noble families of the kingdom of Kosala resided- rarely ceased to amaze Ananda. Today he found no reprieve in its splendour.

Ananda reached for the brass handle of one of the large wooden double doors, and entered the exquisite front room. The floor was covered with intricately patterned woven mats and rugs. Lifelike statues made from clay, wood, and stone encircled the room. Ananda had been in deep awe of these statues for as long as he could remember. He gazed contemplatively at the statues surrounding him. There were statues of the various Hindu gods and goddesses, heroes and legends of the land, of human beings, animals, images of nature and the divine creation in all of its wondrous forms.

Of all of the statues and sculptures adorning this great quarter of the palace, there was one in particular that drew the affection of the prince. The statue that intrigued Ananda wasn't that of any god or goddess, or any other supernatural being; rather, it was that of a man. The compelling statue of the serene man was perfectly shaped from clay. Ananda walked over and stood adjacent to the life-sized statue of the man who sat cross-legged, with his eyes ever slightly closed. His hands rested in his lap, right over left, and his palms were facing upward. Ananda observed the man's countenance with a sense of adulation. The sculptor had given form to the beauty of this man who dwelt in all-pervading tranquility. It became clear to Ananda that the man portrayed in the statue expressed unlimited compassion for all beings. It was as if this man, the prince Siddhartha who had come to be known as Gautama the Buddha, held the welfare of all sentient beings ever so closely to his heart. The title of the Buddha was an honour meaning the one who has awakened, and Ananda remembered hearing a story about the Buddha that epitomized the true meaning of this title.

The Buddha walked slowly and consciously through a village when a man by the roadside stopped him to ask a question. The Buddha, with his warm countenance and balanced demeanour, enraptured the man.

The man was smitten and asked: "Excuse me Venerable Sir, are you one of the gods?"

"No sir," the Buddha answered.

"Venerable Sir, then are you an angel?" the man asked.

"No sir," the Buddha replied.

"Venerable Sir, are you a *gandharva*, a celestial musician?" the man asked, now perplexed.

"No sir," the Buddha replied once more.

"Venerable Sir, then are you a demon?" the man inquired hesitantly.

"No sir," the Buddha replied.

"Oh, Venerable Sir, who or what are you then?" asked the man.

The Buddha smiled, gazed deeply into the man's eyes, and replied with the same calm and tranquility as he had each time.

"Dear Sir, I am awake," he said.

Ananda enjoyed the insight this story provided. It demonstrated that one who has awakened was higher than the angels and even the gods. Prior to his enlightenment, the Buddha was but an ordinary man, thus further illustrating that all beings had the capacity to awaken. It illustrated that all beings inherently possessed *Buddha-nature*, the capacity to become a Buddha. The story of the Enlightened One clearly demonstrated that Siddhartha had found the path that led to his awakening, and that all beings not only have the capacity, but the duty, to awaken, to discover and tread the path leading to their own awakening. Ananda was now ready to embark on the journey of awakening.

CHAPTER 2

Ananda spent many days of his youth in an exquisite flower garden lined with exotic trees bearing bountiful fruits. The young prince enjoyed resting underneath the shade of these trees, and was often accompanied by his companion Keshava.

On one particular occasion, the two of them were alone in the garden, and Ananda was in a particularly loquacious mood.

"You know that I have long since been disillusioned with many aspects of the Holy Vedas," Ananda said, "particularly with their glorification of war and animal sacrifice. However, what really disturbs me the most is the fact that the only people who are allowed to possess the knowledge of the Vedas, of their sacrifices and austerities, are the Brahmin priests. It is my firm conviction that true spiritual practice should be made available to all. There is no man, woman, or child for whom spirituality should not be directly accessible; there is none for whom an intermediary should be necessary in order to access the highest wisdom that rests within their own hearts. The role of the priest as intermediary between a person and their higher self is of great disturbance to me, and any spiritual practice that is of this nature should be immediately refuted. I do, however, find truth and wisdom in the teachings of the Upanishads."

Keshava nodded. The Upanishads were spiritual treatises that were written by rogue yogis who themselves were disillusioned with the Vedas. The glory of the Upanishads was that its spirit rested in love, harmony, and the unity of all creation.

"There is, indeed, great beauty and meaning to be found in the verses of the Upanishads," Keshava replied. "Take the following passage for instance: 'The one who sees all beings in their own Self, and their own Self in all beings, loses all fear. When a sage sees this great Unity and their Self has become all beings, what delusion and what sorrow can ever be near them?' This passage embodies the central tenet of the Upanishads that the perception of unity is the gateway leading to the end of all suffering."

"This central tenet is a precursor to Buddhism," Ananda replied. "The Buddha, himself, had been an ardent student of the Upanishads. However, the Buddha extrapolated on the teachings of the Upanishads, on the best of the teachings that were laid out before him, and merged them with his own experience and insight to form the *dharma*. The Buddha was able to walk along the paths that had been previously laid out, and he followed them until they led him to his own path. It is for this reason that the teachings of the Buddha appeal to me. I have found a kindred spirit in this man. His virtue and integrity are worthy of emulation."

Keshava hesitated for a moment, the question that he was about to ask surely violated every rule of the caste system; yet, he knew that their friendship was stronger than any such divisive force.

"Permit me to ask you a question," Keshava said. "As of late, I have begun to notice certain changes in your behaviour. You have grown increasingly reclusive. Are you going to leave the princely life to seek out a path of asceticism?"

"Rather than myself seeking out a path of asceticism, I feel that when the time is right a path of asceticism will find me of its own accord," Ananda replied. "The winds of change are blowing and the seasons of my life are in transition. Everything has had its purpose. Every single experience of my life to date has shaped my character and formed my destiny. This has been the cause and effect of my life. Every cause has had its effect and the subsequent effect has been the cause for another effect. This has been my *karma*. My karma is spurring me forward."

"Have you, then, already made plans for your departure?" Keshava asked.

The question itself was a statement.

"I have had premonitions of the path that waits ahead," Ananda continued. "Now that the path I am to follow has been imagined and conceived it is only a matter of time before the outer world manifests it into reality. This is something that I have learned time and time again, whenever there has been a calling of my inner voice, an exigency of my soul, the outer world has always manifested the opportunity for this calling to be answered. It has never failed, and I am certain that it will not fail again. My inner voice is calling once more, and it is only a matter of time before the outer world beckons forth with its response."

Keshava gazed at his companion through devout eyes. From his perspective there was no higher god worth serving than this noble youth who was the heir to the throne of Kosala. Since Ananda's birth it had been no secret that the prince was a special individual. The circumstances surrounding his birth had an ethereal quality about them. Several days after Ananda was born, when the festivities were at their climax, a visit was made to the palace by a group of austere men and women adorned in bright saffron robes patterned after rice fields. These monks and nuns were known to be members of the *sangha*, or Buddhist community.

The searing sun reflected its rays off of the cleanly shaven heads of the monks and nuns as they approached the palace. They walked in a deliberate manner, each step carefully measured. They carried large iron bowls in front of them. The citizens placed their hands together in front of their chests and bowed before the members of the sangha. The king and queen, too, bowed before the holy men and women upon their entrance to the palace. The monk in the centre of the procession approached the royalty and requested permission to see the newborn prince. Both the king and queen understood that this particular man was highly realized and thus they granted the man's wish without a moment of hesitation.

The queen bowed slightly, smiling, as she handed the precious baby boy to the monk. Neither holy man nor baby made a sound or gesture as the two traded gazes replete with love and wisdom. For several silent moments the holy man gazed into the depths of the eyes of the baby Ananda. The entire assembly was silently waiting in eager anticipation.

"I am honoured to have had the presence of the baby prince Ananda bestowed upon me," the holy man said.

"I have been touched by the highest grace. In this baby, the child Ananda, I have seen one who is destined for the ultimate greatness."

"Greatness?" the king replied, unable to hide his jubilant smile. "Do you not speak of the sort of greatness that befits a king, or, perhaps, even an emperor?"

"No," the holy man replied, giving the king a look of stern consternation. "It concerns nothing of the sort. It concerns the journey, and the end of the journey. Ananda is destined for the ultimate greatness, that of reaching the end of the journey. He will bring a grinding halt to the wheel of *samsara*. Ananda will realize *nirvana* in this very lifetime."

The king was immobilized. Samsara? What good was the end of samsara? This was not the wish he had for his son. He fell mute and watched as the holy man kissed the baby Ananda on the forehead and handed him back to his mother. The shining monk then bowed reverently before the baby, before the royalty, before the assembly, and the sangha turned around, leaving the palace as peacefully as they had arrived.

The young prince Ananda was unable to ascertain which astounded him more: the lifelike quality of his dreams or the dreamlike quality of his life. At night he dreamt vividly; he experienced his dreams in as real a fashion as anything he experienced while awake. He remembered his dreams with great clarity and detail. Meanwhile, his life seemed to be woven from the same illusory fabric as his dreams. Nothing in the manifest world was quite tangible. It was all *maya*. It was a world of illusions.

After the day's events with Keshava, Ananda lay awake in his bed in the royal chambers, unable to sleep. The longing within him was stirring. The sapling in his soul, whose seed had been planted long ago, was now sprouting voraciously. Finally, after lying awake for quite some time, he fell into a deep sleep and had a mysterious dream.

In the dream, he was wandering around the palace grounds, and found himself in the courtyard alone. The entire palace was desolate, not even the wind stirred in the slightest. He walked down to the riverbank, and much to his chagrin, he found no one there either. Suddenly, he felt an acute loneliness that he had never experienced before, whether awake or dreaming.

He continued walking and entered the palace, yet it was vacant, utterly barren. Finally, he slumped down to the ground and sat in one of the palace halls. As his sense of loneliness was climaxing, his mother entered the room laughing.

Ananda rose and approached her. Strangely, she did not seem to notice him. The queen stared straight ahead, oblivious to the presence of her son. Ananda held his mother's hands and gazed into her eyes. She was not aware of him in the least; he no longer seemed to exist to her. The queen then walked straight out of the hall and into an adjacent corridor.

At that moment, Ananda's father entered the hallway. Ananda thankfully approached his father and hugged him. Yet the king, too, strangely, was completely unaware of his son's presence. He continued walking straight down the hallway and exited from the same corridor from which his wife had departed earlier. It was as if Ananda had been a mere apparition.

Ananda awoke feeling frightened and puzzled. The solitary nature of the human condition had thrust itself upon him, revealed through his dream. Every human being is brought into the world to forge their own path and undertake their own journey. Ananda realized the depth of introspection that was necessary to discover his true nature.

The prince rose from his bed and wandered into the large entrance hall of the palace. He was standing before the statue of that mighty sage, Gautama the Buddha. The austere presence of the Buddha immediately calmed Ananda. The compassion of the Buddha's radiant smile filled the young prince with great comfort. Ananda knew that there could be no greater destiny to follow than to develop his own smile into a smile like the Buddha's, a smile that was entirely perfect in its own regard, a smile that was seeking nothing, lacking nothing. To cultivate such a smile was the highest of paths.

CHAPTER 3

Weeks had now passed since the fateful dream had occurred. Ananda took in the sights, sounds, and smells surrounding him with renewed reverie. The dream had completed a process of leave-taking in his heart; an inward transformation had reached its natural conclusion. A serene sense of detachment was present in his being, a detachment that was entirely liberating, and one that granted him clarity and insight. It was as if, for the first time, he was viewing his life through an unfiltered lens; he was watching himself from above. He now watched his own life through the keen and sharp eyes of a solitary bird perched on the highest treetop in the land.

It was not long before the day arrived when a man wearing a saffron robe arrived at the palace. The man had a cleanly shaven head that reflected the brilliant sunlight, and he carried a large iron bowl in front of him. Ananda was enjoying a moment of solitude beneath a tree in the flower garden, when he felt a wave of energy rush through him, looked up, and spotted the man. The young prince recognized this man to be a Buddhist monk and his heart rejoiced at the sight. Ananda studied the elderly man. Despite the monk's age, his features bore radiant youth and vitality, enchanting Ananda with their presence. Each step the man took was deliberate, centred in peace and awareness. Through the man's countenance Ananda understood that this man was the most realized human being that he had ever encountered in his life. This, Ananda had understood before either of them had spoken a single word; this he understood through the way the man carried himself with dignified yet humble perfection.

The man was a master of himself, and his smile was imbued with innocence and purity, like that of a child. In relation to the other people that Ananda had met in his life, this man's face shone like moonlight dancing among the stars. The aura that enveloped this monk radiated boundless love and peace.

As the man approached, Ananda placed his hands before his chest and bowed. It was the monk who spoke first. "Dear Prince Ananda, it is a pleasure to make your acquaintance once more."

"Venerable Sir, please forgive my asking," Ananda replied, taken aback. "How is it that you have come to know my name and where have we met before?"

The man smiled. His smile contained enough warmth to melt the ice from the peaks of the Himalayas.

"Although you may remember me not, I remember you well. We first met when you were but a baby, only several days old, and now I have recognized you at once, you have changed very little."

The man laughed heartily as he said this. A wave of familiarity swept through Ananda as a memory from the distant reaches of the past returned to him with striking clarity; he remembered being a baby and staring up into the same radiant eyes into which he now gazed. He remembered it well; rather, he experienced it as if it were happening in the present moment. It was as if that moment from long ago was happening simultaneously with this current moment.

"My name is Kondanna," the monk said.

Ananda felt an ineffable affinity for Kondanna, as if they had known each other before, from a different epoch altogether.

"Yes, I feel it, too," Kondanna said. "We have known each other before."

"How did you do that?" Ananda asked.

"Do what?"

"Read my mind. How did you read my mind?"

The old monk gave a wave of his hand, a gesture indicating the trivial nature of the question.

"When your own mind is clear, it is very easy to read the minds of others," he said. "You will come to learn to clear your mind in time. Meditation is the practice of the stilling of the mind. Once the mind is silent, it is only natural to be able to pick up on the thoughts of others. We all have telepathic abilities; the consciousness of all beings is unified. It is simply a matter of being present."

"Then perhaps, you already know what I am about to say," Ananda replied in a measured tone. "However, I will voice my request nonetheless. I must join you, in order to learn the way. My inner voice is speaking to me. My destiny is unfolding before itself, and I know without a shadow of a doubt that it is my fate to join you in order to learn the way."

Kondanna had been waiting for this day since he had first laid his eyes on the prince as a baby.

"It is for this reason that I have come now. You have summoned me. This inner voice that you speak of is your sacred intuition, and it is wonderful to see that you are already deeply in touch with it. This means that the mind is already quite still. Keep the mind quiet and still. Let it be tranquil like a lake upon which no ripples have formed. When there are no ripples on the surface of the lake, then one is able to see the depths of the lake, and the same premise holds true for the mind.

"Your intuition is your guide along the journey of life. It is this inner voice, and only this inner voice, that you must heed along the way. I, too, know that the time has arrived for you to join us, and it is for this reason that I have been brought here to the palace at this time. We will be blessed and honoured for you to join us, Ananda, and for you to learn the traditions and practices of becoming a *bhikkhu*, a Buddhist monk. Since I am the abbot of the forest grove monastery, you need no further permission from this end. It is now time to seek the blessing of your parents."

Gaining the blessing of his parents to leave the palace and the princely life was a task that would not come easily and, second to taking leave of Keshava, would be the most difficult part of the process. Ananda approached the royal chambers the following morning. He placed his hands in front of his chest, bowed, and then bent down to touch the feet of each of his parents. Performing this gesture showed a great deal of respect towards one's elders.

"I wish to speak with you of some urgent matters," Ananda said, his request rising forth of its own accord. "I have decided to join the sangha. My heart yearns to learn firsthand the teachings of the Buddha."

Deep inside of himself, the king had been expecting something of this nature to happen sooner or later. He was just surprised that it was happening sooner rather than later.

"How can you make such a decision without considering your commitments to the populace?" The king asked. "What of your duties to the kingdom? Surely, you cannot abandon your responsibilities as a prince?"

"It is not because I wish to abandon duty and responsibility that I plan my departure," Ananda replied. "On the contrary, I am following duty and responsibility. I am following the commitments that are calling me from within, that summon me from the heart. I have come to realize that my purpose in life is to follow my intuition, to acquiesce to the callings of my inner voice. I must learn the dharma in order to alleviate the suffering that is prevalent in my own heart. Only once I have liberated myself from the suffering of my own heart can I be of any real service to others. This is the most important task for me to accomplish. In this manner I would be of the greatest service to humanity. I have witnessed the transient nature of all phenomena in this world. I know that the vitality of my youth will soon pass away and then the task will become increasingly difficult."

"What of your duties to family?" The queen asked. "What of your friends here? What about everyone at the palace and in the kingdom? Have you considered them or have you forgotten them?"

"You know that I will always love everyone here. However, my only true duty is towards the calling of my inner voice," Ananda reiterated with great compassion. "Deep within your hearts, you both know that I am right, and that my staying here would no longer be of benefit

to myself or to those around me. Destiny is calling me
forth."

As Ananda spoke these words, images returned to the
king of the holy man who had arrived at the palace shortly
after Ananda's birth. In his heart, the king had always
known that the prophecy of the monk that Ananda was
destined for greatness beyond that of kingship would
come to manifest itself in some manner, and it was now
happening right before his eyes. The king knew that the
proper course of action would be for him to allow his son
to leave, yet he would not relent.

"Ananda," the king said, measuring each word as if the
fate of the universe hung in their balance. "I think that
you should be reasonable and reconsider your decision.
You are of royal descent and you are destined to be king.
This is your destiny, to be a king. Your destiny is that of
royalty, nobility, and greatness."

"Father, look into my eyes. Please take a moment to
look into my eyes."

The king stared into the deep wellspring of Ananda's
brown eyes where he saw resolute conviction balanced
with limitless compassion. The king's gaze remained fixed
on the eyes of his son for several moments, moments that
lasted lifetimes. He now knew, beyond a shadow of a
doubt, that the time had come for him to let his son go.
The time had come to open the door of the cage and
allow the golden bird to soar.

"I, too, realize that there is no longer any place for you
here," the king said, he gazed at his wife who reluctantly
nodded her head. "When you were a baby, a holy man,
a Buddhist monk, came to the palace and it was his
prophecy that you would not become king. Today, we

will finally accept what we have refused to accept for so long. You must follow the voice of your heart as it speaks to you. If the desire to become king should ever return to you, then the throne remains. The gates of this palace, and the gateway to our hearts, will always remain open to you. You have our blessing to join the sangha."

Chapter 4

An extensive variety of flora and fauna flourished in the forest grove monastery. Majestic banyans, towering papals, bamboo, birch, and fig trees surrounded the grove, offering comfort, security, and peace to the environment within. Brightly coloured, fresh scented orchids, lilies, jasmines, and daisies bloomed throughout the monastery. The trees and plants in the grove all shared another characteristic with one another, and this was a characteristic that did not go unnoticed by Ananda. They were all full of abundant vitality; they all possessed an extraordinary power of attraction, a distinct beauty that was uncommon to trees and plants elsewhere.

In the distance, the gentle rushing of the river could be heard. This sound was often joined in the early mornings by the songs of joyous blackbirds and robins. Squirrels scampered this way and that, often pausing for a rest on a tree branch. Rabbits hopped along until they found a place to sit and dwell in contemplative awareness. Thatched huts lined the edge of the forest and encircled the monastery within the austere grove. Although the grove was secluded in the heart of the forest, it remained close enough to several villages where the monastic community would proceed on their daily alms rounds to accept food offerings from the lay people.

Ananda took in the sights and sounds of his environment with heightened wonder. Several dozen monks and nuns, all clad in shaven heads and saffron robes, were either seated motionless, and immersed in meditation, or were walking mindfully about the perimeter of the grove with their feet kissing the earth with every step they took. One trait that all of these bhikkhus and *bhikkhunis* shared was that they each possessed, in varying degrees, an unwavering sense of inward serenity. They each possessed a deep smile that they shared not only with each other but, also, with the vibrant landscape of this austere residence.

As an ordained bhikkhu, Ananda was required to shave his head, take refuge in the triple gems of the Buddha, the dharma, and the sangha, and to follow two-hundred-and-twenty-seven precepts. Of these precepts, the first five were considered to be of the utmost importance for living a harmonious life. They were to vow to refrain from killing or causing injury to any living being, from taking that which is not freely given, from performing acts of sexual misconduct, from harsh and false speech, and to vow to refrain from taking intoxicating liquor and drugs.

Ananda soundlessly joined the group of monks and nuns who were practicing walking meditation in an extremely slow, and, seemingly exaggerated, manner. Ananda gently raised one leg from the ground; paused in mid-air before extending and straightening that leg out in front of him, and then paused again before lowering the leg to softly touch the ground. As he continued walking in this manner, a profound sense of tranquility came over him. His thoughts and emotions dwindled and then vanished; he became incredibly alive, and immersed in the present moment. As the movements of his body slowed down, so the mind followed. All notions of time had fallen away entirely. All that remained was the infinite depth of the present moment during which he was kissing the earth softly with his feet.

The early morning was cool and crisp, the grass wet with dew, and a light mist hung in the air. The birds sang harmoniously as they rested on their perches. The crickets chirped praise to the gift of another morning, and an air of renewal permeated the grove. Ananda and Kondanna were walking mindfully through a forest path.

"How do you feel now that you have officially renounced princely life and taken on the discipline of a bhikkhu?" Kondanna asked. "Do you feel like you have lost your freedom in some way? Do you feel like you have taken on shackles?"

Ananda knew that Kondanna was testing him. "To the ordinary person this type of discipline would certainly seem like the voluntary taking on of shackles," he replied. "This type of renunciation would certainly seem like the entire restriction of one's freedom. However, rather than restricting my freedom, practicing this type of discipline provides boundless freedom. The ordinary person would consider freedom to be the ability to pursue their desires. In reality this concept of freedom is quite limiting, and is not freedom at all, for one is bound to endless desire; they are shackled to the wheel of samsara. By taking the precepts, and accepting the discipline that accompanies them, I am providing myself the highest freedom. I am providing myself freedom *from* my endless desires and the inherent suffering they entail. This newfound freedom that I am being given, by my own choice to live consciously, is liberating me from being a slave to the constant grasping of the mind. Happiness requires a light-hearted discipline. Of the people I have met in my life, it is those who have had this gentle yet unwavering form of discipline that have been the happiest without exception."

"You are learning well," Kondanna replied, his renowned smile forming once more on his face, brightening the landscape around them.

Every fortnight, during the evenings at the grove, one of the members of the sangha would give a dharma talk, a discourse pertaining to one of the many teachings of the Buddha. Lay people from the surrounding villages would come to the monastery to join the bhikkhus and bhikkhunis in hearing the dharma talks.

On this particular occasion, Kondanna's eyes, and his entire being, shone with impeccable radiance.

"The Four Noble Truths are the bedrock of the Buddha's teaching," he began. "It is these truths that form the backbone of the dharma. While many of us here today are familiar with these truths, it is important to occasionally clarify our perceptions of that which we already know.

"The first noble truth is that there is *dukkha*, or suffering. It is that suffering exists. When the Brahmin priests, Vedic scholars, and other detractors of the Buddha's teachings hear this first noble truth they immediately accuse the dharma of being nihilistic. However, we all know that nothing could be further from the truth; life is, indeed, fraught with suffering. Life is full of obvious sufferings such as sickness and disease, pain and death. Even if one is young and healthy, without proper perception they, too, are suffering. For, the body that is young and healthy is transient. It is subject to the waves of impermanence like anything else in the world, and every one of us will become old or sick, and die in some manner. How many elderly people have you known that cherished the memories of their youth as valuable keepsakes, living vicariously through a past existence that the ocean of time has long since washed away?

"Moreover, people who are healthy in body are often afflicted in the mind. They suffer from anxiety or worry, a lack of meaning or purpose, and they search the manifest world for happiness. They search endlessly but do not find what they seek. They search until they have traversed ocean and land alike, until they have climbed the highest mountaintop and descended the lowest valley. Everything they encounter is changing; it is all transient. Yet, they find some temporary happiness in one thing or another, and they cling to this object of pleasure, hoping to find some lasting satisfaction there within. They squeeze every last drop of nectar until the bittersweet fruit can give no more. Furthermore, once they have become separated from their object of happiness, then their suffering increases manifold. After the loss of their happiness has occurred- and this is inevitably bound to occur- they are now searching for a new object of happiness to alleviate their suffering. They are searching for one more bittersweet fruit in which even a single drop of nectar still remains. This is the nature of samsara. This is the nature of wandering on! The Buddha once asked his disciples the following question, 'Which of these do you think is greater, all of the water in all of the oceans of the world or the accumulation of tears that you have shed while wandering on?' Of course, we all know the answer to that question.

"The second noble truth, then, follows directly from the first. The second noble truth is that there is a cause of suffering. The cause of suffering is the perception that that which is impermanent may bring us permanent happiness. The Buddha said, 'Let us be like islands that no flood can engulf.' He taught us to take refuge within ourselves. The happiness that dwells in our hearts cannot be subject to external circumstances! If we place our capacity for happiness in anything outside of us, if we attach our capacity for happiness to anything external, then we are bound to suffer. We are bound to suffer because the object to which we have attached our capacity for happiness is going to leave or change in some way or another, at some time or another, and then we will be most unhappy.

"It is precisely at this juncture that the detractors of the dharma are certain they have found the flaw in the teachings of the Enlightened One. They say that if one practices non-attachment all of the time, how can one love? Where does one find the capacity to love another person in the doctrine of the Buddha? If one is not attached to anything, then how can compassion exist?"

At this point Kondanna laughed, as did the assembly before him, including Ananda. The former prince was able to foresee the direction in which Kondanna was heading.

"Know this within the innermost depths of your being," Kondanna continued. "Attachment is not love! Attachment causes suffering. It causes suffering both to the one who is attached, and to the one who is the recipient of this attachment. The suffering exists as such because when one is attached they only see other people and things in relation to their own self. The only way, and I emphasize only, to truly love anyone or anything is

26

without attachment; the only way to love something is to allow it to express its own true nature. We love that for which it is, for nothing more and nothing less than what it is naturally. Once we have established non-attachment, it is then that we are in a position to develop unconditional love. In order to radiate unconditional love, we must develop a great degree of equanimity within ourselves, and it is here that the noble virtue of non-attachment rides in on its eloquent horse. The Buddha said to love all beings with a boundless heart, just as a mother would love her only child. Oh, think of how the mother loves all of her children! It is with this degree of courage that we must love all beings."

It was becoming ever clearer to Ananda that the words Kondanna spoke came directly from the wise old monk's own experience, and that life itself had been Kondanna's greatest teacher. Every word that Kondanna spoke reached Ananda with striking clarity. It was as if these words were coming from the very depths of Ananda's own being, and were being articulated to him through the abbot of the community.

Kondanna continued, precisely measuring each word that he spoke. "The third noble truth then follows directly from the previous two. The third noble truth is that there is an end to dukkha, a cessation of suffering. The cessation of suffering can begin once a shift in perception has occurred. This perceptual shift is in accordance with a sound understanding of the first two noble truths. It involves letting go and acceptance. Once we are able to let go of our attachments, our cravings and desires as well as our aversions and fears, then we are in a position to accept things as they truly are. In order to accept the nature of things as they are, we must become fully present to this moment. We must experience this moment exactly as it is. Our minds are continually oscillating between thoughts of the past and thoughts of the future. This continual oscillation is the very nature of the mind. The mind requires both the past and the future in order to create cravings and desires, aversions and fears. The mind thrives on past and future, and in fact, it can *only* exist in relation to them. The mind does not exist in this moment. In the present moment, where is the mind? The Buddha was once asked why his disciples were so radiant and joyful. His answer was that they were so radiant and joyful because they did not dwell in the past, nor brood over the future. They were so radiant and joyful because they lived fully and deeply in the present moment. This is the third noble truth that there is an end to suffering."

Ananda admired the way that Kondanna had set himself up to give the fourth noble truth, and was now eager, as was the rest of the assembly, to hear the abbot's discourse on the final of the four noble truths.

Kondanna continued with mindfulness. "The question then becomes how exactly does one proceed to bring about the cessation of suffering? This is the central question of the dharma, and ultimately, it is the central question of the spiritual path. While the third noble truth told us that dukkha could be brought to an end, the fourth noble truth provides us with a clear path for ending this suffering. Thus, the fourth noble truth is that there is a path that leads to the end of suffering, and it is known as the Noble Eightfold Path. The Eightfold Path stems from awareness and compassion. If we are aware, fully and deeply aware of the present moment, then we will naturally perform the most fruitful action in any and every given moment. If we have cultivated compassion within our hearts, then our intentions will be pure and we will not strive to harm or to overtake another. Our actions will then follow suit to be compassionate in their nature.

"Awareness and compassion are as intertwined as the spider and the web that it spins. We cannot have one without the other. We may conceive ourselves to be compassionate, but if we are not fully aware and mindful of our actions, then despite our good intentions we will bring harm upon ourselves and other beings. We will not be able to help this. No matter how hard we try it will not make a difference; since we are lacking awareness, we do not *know* what we are doing. In the same manner, if we are truly aware, then compassion is the necessary companion to our awareness. One who is truly mindful would not willfully bring harm or suffering upon any other living being. Hence, compassion and awareness are necessarily intertwined and by cultivating these two virtues we are now on our way to bringing about the cessation of suffering."

The old monk fell silent, and as he did so there was complete silence in the grove; nature itself had fallen silent. Kondanna then raised his head, gazed across the assembly before him and said: "Let us practice *maitri-bhavana*, loving-kindness meditation, to cultivate compassion and awareness in our hearts, and wish happiness upon all beings."

CHAPTER 5

The bell resonated well before daybreak, its deep pitch echoing throughout the forest monastery. The entire sangha sat on their cushions, made from tightly packed bundles of fragrant *kusa* grass, and practiced meditation. Ananda crossed his legs and assumed *padmasana*, the lotus posture. This posture was called as such as it imitated the figure of a blooming lotus. He closed his eyes, sat perfectly motionless, breathing in the serenity of the morning. The meditation technique that he had learned from Kondanna, and, indeed, the technique that all of the monks and nuns here at the grove practiced, was also the one that the Buddha was believed to have used when he attained enlightenment under the *bodhi* tree. This technique was called *anapana-sati*, or mindfulness of breathing.

Ananda observed his breath as it entered and exited his nostrils. He observed the breathing process with one-pointed attention, as it occurred naturally, without attempting to coerce the breath in any way. First, he would breathe in, his entire awareness resting with this in-breath, allowing the breath to be effortless. After the in-breath had finished, and before the next out-breath had begun, there was a space. Ananda allowed his awareness to rest in this space between the in-breath and the out-breath. He then observed the out-breath. It was slow and gentle, as calm as the morning breeze. After the out-breath had finished, he allowed his awareness to rest in the space between out-breath and in-breath. He continued to follow this procedure of breathing in, noticing the space, breathing out, and noticing the space again, immersing himself in its harmonious rhythm.

As he focused on the breath, various thoughts would enter his mind. When he became aware that a thought had entered his mind, he acknowledged the thought and returned his awareness to the breath. Pleasant and unpleasant thoughts alike entered into his mind, and each time that a thought arose, he observed its presence with perfect equanimity, and then gently returned his awareness to the breath. Time after time, a thought would come, and then it would go. A subtle yet profound realization came to Ananda, all of the thoughts and emotions in his mind, no matter how pleasant or unpleasant they were, came and went. There was no thought that would stay permanently in his mind. Thoughts and emotions were elusively fleeting, coming and going of their own accord, arising and passing like the waves in the river.

As these thoughts occurred to him, a strange thing happened. He naturally entered into a state of emptiness, a state of perfect clarity. He entered into a distinct space that exists when one thought has finished, and before another thought has arisen. He entered a state where he was entirely mindful. He now realized that to dwell in this space was, indeed, the essence of meditation practice. As soon as he noticed a thought arise, Ananda swiftly and diligently observed its presence, released it, and returned his awareness to the breath, entering once more into the gap. While resting in this gap he was acutely aware of the present moment, and the frequency of his thoughts diminished. Essentially, the gap was getting wider. The space between the thoughts was expanding, becoming a cavity of supreme bliss.

The bell rang once more, sounding the end of meditation practice. Ananda opened his eyes and gazed at the trees ahead of him. They appeared brighter and greener than before, and the flowers seemed more lucid and full of colour, their fragrance more pleasant. Everything around him was vivid, attractive, and beautiful. Every single thing upon which he looked was alive with a fresh sense of both elegance and purpose, and every single living organism played its exact role within the complex web that was the interplay of life. He looked upon his surroundings with the innocent wonder of a child, a child to whom everything is beautiful and sacred, to whom every bird and branch, fig and flower, contains its own secret deep in its heart. It is within this very secret, that the mystery of life itself lies.

The procession of monks and nuns gracefully approached the village on their daily alms round, in order to beg for their single meal. A group of excited young children were awaiting the procession at the village entrance. They placed their hands before their chests, knelt and bowed as the sangha drew nearer. The children began to give them handfuls of sticky rice, as well as fresh fruits and vegetables. The procession continued farther into the village where the adults, too, offered food to the monastic community.

Ananda gazed at the many men, women, and children sitting and standing outside of their thatched huts, offering alms. Ananda could not help but feel deep compassion for the plight of all sentient beings. He could not help but notice not only the suffering of the elderly and infirm, the suffering of the poor and impoverished, but also the suffering of the young and healthy, and of the rich and wealthy. He saw the inherent suffering of a strong young man who was attached to his youth and strength, and the inherent suffering of a beautiful maiden clinging to her charm. Every flower that bloomed in the springtime would fade and wither as autumn departed, and winter arrived. If people were aware of the inevitable transience of all things, then they could easily make strides towards the cessation of suffering before it even happened. When the mind is pointed in the right direction it will reach the destination of its own accord, just as an arrow that is well aimed pierces its target once released from the bow.

At nightfall, Ananda approached Kondanna and discussed his experience of the alms round earlier that day.

"When we were walking through the village, I was overcome with a tremendous magnitude of sympathy and compassion for all of life," Ananda said. "I felt the pain of all sentient beings, beings spending lifetime after lifetime senselessly wandering on, treading the wheel of samsara, with no thoughts of liberation, no awareness of the unity of all of life; I felt this suffering as if it were my very own."

The wise abbot eyed his pupil. "Suffering is inherent from the moment of birth," Kondanna answered. "It is the illusion of separateness that is the root cause of all suffering. We are like islands in a vast sea, we perceive ourselves to be separate and distinct, but underneath the vast sea of maya, all of the bodies of land are connected and are one great body of land."

"How many lifetimes do humans spend, and will they continue to spend, wandering on?" Ananda asked, as he gazed into the distance. "How many births and deaths will be spent continuing this senseless pursuit of pleasure and pain, of desires and aversions? These people play the game of samsara like eager children; over and over, they are all too willing to immerse themselves once more in the hands of pleasure and pain. How can one be content to continue running in circles like a hamster on a wheel? No, it is not a desirable fate to ceaselessly continue playing this game of samsara. Lifetime after lifetime spent in endless pursuit of the elusive dream of happiness, a happiness that is always just out of reach, just around the next corner. Oh, how long can one remain fully immersed in samsara?"

Kondanna knew that, ultimately, Ananda would not find the answers to his questions while living at the monastery.

Chapter 6

The torrential downpour of the monsoon season came and went, giving way to the cool winters, in turn yielding to the blooming springs and searing summer days. In this manner, the cycle of seasons turned several times over, and in what seemed but a moment's time, Ananda had spent six full years living within the forest grove monastery. He had grasped the sacred teachings of the Buddha with unparalleled ease. The felicity with which he learned had astonished the entire sangha. Ananda now gave dharma talks that were full of ineffable depth and that contained the jewels of his own experiential understanding. People from all over the land flocked in droves to the forest grove monastery in order to hear this brilliant young monk speak.

Ananda had long since become a master of meditation. He was able to spend days on end observing the breath with unwavering diligence. His counsel was often sought by many of the elder and more experienced monks and nuns, as well as novices, for advice on their own practice. He answered each in turn with perfect equanimity and love, providing them with the exact answer- whether through words, gestures, or silence- that they needed in that given moment. His mind had become incredibly clear. Thoughts rarely entered, and his inner voice was impeccably discernable.

On the rare occasion that a thought entered, and his mind began to wander, he returned his awareness to the present moment and to that glorious space in between thoughts with swiftness and ease. He knew that this space was available to him at all times- the space in between thoughts where past and future had dissolved entirely, and had entered into the chasm of now. This space was there at all times, and at all times the present moment yielded the opportunity for the practice of mindfulness. Just as the river did not lament over past actions nor dwell over future outcomes but continued to flow unremittingly, so too did Ananda's mind maintain present moment awareness without slackening.

The relationship between Kondanna and Ananda, between teacher and disciple, had blossomed and borne exquisite fruit. Ananda revered Kondanna greatly, and listened with care and attention to the words of wisdom that the elder monk spoke. In the abbot, Ananda had found a man whose every step promoted peace, every word spoke of harmony, and whose every gesture was full of grace. Ananda cherished the noble and dignified character of the elderly monk and, as was evident to anyone that observed the pair, he held this teacher and sage ever close to his heart. Their relationship was also of greater worth to Kondanna than Ananda could have ever possibly imagined.

Kondanna esteemed Ananda's countenance above all else. Nothing pleased the wise old monk more than watching the graceful manner in which Ananda took each purposeful step. Kondanna admired the way Ananda sat perfectly strong yet still in meditation, as if neither a giant nor a torrent could move this statuesque form and cause its balanced mind to waver in the least. The abbot was enchanted when listening to Ananda giving dharma talks in his musical voice and poetic language. The way that Ananda grasped the teachings of the Buddha while making them his own was unparalleled to any other bhikkhu or bhikkhuni that Kondanna had ever observed.

Ananda intently observed the other monks and nuns around him. Some were seated and immersed in meditation, while others walked mindfully. Ananda loved these people dearly. He had never met a group of more highly realized beings. These were the most awakened people whose presence he had been blessed with during his life. Ananda realized, however, that he could no longer walk the sacred path of the Buddha. Rather, he was required to forge his own path, and to blaze his own trail. This required Ananda to cease being a Buddhist, in order that he may become a Buddha, a fully awakened being.

Living in the forest grove had certainly been fruitful. Practicing and studying the Buddha's teachings was the highest of blessings bestowed upon him. He had developed a sound routine of meditation, mindfulness, and living in communion with nature. There was a sense of comfort that the grove provided its' residents. It was, however, precisely this sense of comfort that was beginning to disturb Ananda. He was, in fact, becoming too comfortable. His inner voice was rising once more; it was informing him that he was beginning to lose his ardour and zealousness.

He had not told anyone, not even Kondanna, of the premonitions he had been having. This was the first secret that he had ever kept from the abbot. The premonitions had begun some time ago as vague intimations and had gradually developed into intense longings. He knew that he would recognize her immediately when they met, and that they would, indeed, meet again in this lifetime. She had been the tree that grew next to him; they had grown in each other's shadows. Her branches intertwined with his. She was the fox with whom he playfully nestled on the forest floor. She was the elegant dove who soared by his side across many a horizon. She was the fish with whom he swam endless oceans. She had been the star with whom he danced in many a night sky, together delighting the heavens. She accompanied him in many human incarnations as his lover and friend. She had been there a thousand times and would be there once again. Just as Yasodhara and Siddhartha had been companions many times over she, too, would return to join Ananda.

Ananda closed his eyes but for a moment to meditate when a familiar figure sat down next to him. Kondanna caressed a bright yellow daisy in his hand and stroked it as he spoke. "There is something stirring within you, your inner voice is rising once again," the abbot said with certainty.

"You are, indeed, correct," Ananda replied, he would never cease to be amazed at the accuracy with which Kondanna had always been able to read his mind. "At one time life here in the monastery had provided me with fervent enthusiasm, yet now this enthusiasm has waned. More than this, however, I am becoming attached to the lifestyle here in the grove. I am realizing that I have become attached not only to the grove, its surroundings and members, but also to the very concept of being a monk itself."

Kondanna gazed ever deeper into the starry eyes of his pupil. It was with this gaze of unlimited compassion and understanding that he knew Ananda's decision had been made, and that it had, in fact, been made long ago. He had observed Ananda's countenance with great care and scrutiny, and the destiny of this young monk had long since been written in his eyes, in his walk, and in his every movement and mannerism. Kondanna understood that the best way to love this glorious bird was to open the door of the cage, in order that it may fly away of its own volition.

"There really is no such thing as a Buddhist, for then it would be undesirable to be a Buddhist," Kondanna said. "There are only awakened beings and those on the journey to awakening. A Buddhist is one who in some way or another has formed attachment to the teachings of the original Buddha. One can be a student of the Buddha, an ardent and devoted student of the Buddha, but one should never carry the label or guise of being a Buddhist. Names and labels only cause separation and division, while the teachings of the Buddha were of perfect unity. The Buddha, himself, would have never wanted Buddhists.

"He would not have wanted a cult of followers who took his every word as gospel, or ceased to have the ability to think for themselves and act of their own volition. He is known to have urged his disciples to not believe a single word that he spoke if it did not accord with their own experience. Then it is no longer a matter of belief but a matter of knowing. He would have only wanted others to awaken, to discover their own Buddha-nature, to allow the flowers of enlightenment already inherent within them to blossom. Thinking oneself to be a Buddhist requires a certain amount of attachment to the teachings of the Buddha. Yet, the very teachings of the Buddha require one to find their own way, to forge their own path. In order to find enlightenment, the Buddha had to go his own way. He had to leave all established doctrines behind. Despite your prowess in meditation, you are still far from this goal."

"I have, indeed, learned the highest of teachings," Ananda replied, he understood that Kondanna spoke out of boundless compassion. "In my entire life I have never encountered a doctrine that was as full of piercing depth into the nature of existence as that of the dharma. There is no other system of philosophy or practice that eclipses the teachings of the Buddha. In renouncing the path of the Buddha, I am now renouncing all paths. In coming to the end of the trails left behind by others, I will now be able to find my own trail. Further, I have been blessed with the opportunity to practice with a learned master, a teacher whose realization of the nature of life itself is second to none amongst all that I have met in my lifetime."

Ananda knew that his parting would carry its share of grief both for himself and for all of those bhikkhus and bhikkhunis who were dear to him just as his parting from his childhood home had caused its own fair share of grief. Yet, he had been right to leave then, and knew that he would be right once more. These wounds of grief would soon heal and, in time, blossom into beautiful flowers of the heart. For, the master alchemist of time heals all wounds, no matter how deep they may be. The image of the river returned to Ananda once more, the image of the waves arising and passing. The time had come for him to seek new beginnings.

Ananda rose at dawn on his last day as a monk and decided to walk in the forest glade. Seemingly out of nowhere, a small and beautiful bird, a gray and black robin, landed at his feet. Ananda laughed cheerfully. The bird chirped its merry reply, and then hopped several feet in front of the young monk. Ananda walked in his slow and measured pace to where the robin was now resting, and when he reached the bird, it again hopped several feet in front of him. Ananda continued walking to where the bird would rest, and it would in turn continue to hop several feet in front of him, or flutter to a low hanging tree branch until Ananda had caught up to its new position.

In this manner, Ananda playfully followed the bird through the forest. He had walked a considerable distance from the monastery when shafts of light from the morning sun were beginning to filter through the forest canopy high above. It would now be time for meditation, yet the bird continued to play this game unremittingly, and the familiar voice within Ananda's heart told him to keep playing along as well. Finally, the robin landed on a branch at a clearing near the edge of the forest, rose up, and flew away. Ananda walked straight to the papal tree where the bird had been perched a moment ago and, as if in a dream, gazed through the clearing that lay before him.

The beautiful young woman wore a flowing long blue sari. She was practicing *hatha yoga* on the riverbank. The movements of her supple limbs were as graceful as those of a gazelle. The natural beauty of this woman struck a chord in the harp that was the heart of the young monk, it was not only an outward beauty that struck him so, although her beauty eclipsed that of any woman that Ananda had encountered in his life; rather, it was an inward beauty, a radiant essence that shone from the depths of her soul that enchanted Ananda. Her beauty was wholesome and pure, soothing to the gaze like all good things of the earth. In a similar manner to gazing at flowers, trees, lakes, and stars, gazing at this woman imbued Ananda with joy.

The young woman slowly turned around, sensing she was being watched, and looked directly up at the handsome monk who stood motionless watching her. Their eyes locked for a moment during which the hands of time stood still. The woman then walked slowly towards the monk, placed her hands before her chest, and bowed before him in the customary manner. Ananda placed his hands before his chest and bowed in return, smiling at the wondrous sight that his eyes now beheld.

"Forgive me Venerable," the woman said. Her voice was soft and harmonious, the type that is usually reserved for songbirds. "I have no alms to offer you at this time."

Upon speaking these words she could not help but notice the childlike beauty of this man. She felt an incredible affinity for him, as if she had known him before.

"This is of no concern," Ananda replied. "The universe provides me with exactly that which I need, whenever I need it. If you wish, however, you may offer your name in place of the customary alms."

A radiant smile formed on the woman's face.

"My name is Anjali," she said.

Ananda raised his right hand above her head.

"My dear Anjali, I grant you many blessings. It has been a pleasure to make your acquaintance. My name is Ananda."

Anjali laughed, her joyous laugh melting the core of the monk's being.

"Thank you, Ananda," she said softly.

The enchanted pair took a long parting glance at one another. They entered each other's being through their eyes, the windows of their souls, and then bid each other farewell. They travelled in opposite directions with Ananda returning to the forest grove.

Chapter 7

Ananda had spent days treading through the dirt paths and dense underbrush of the forest. Kondanna had performed the disrobing ceremony in private, and Ananda had returned his alms bowl, his razor, and his three saffron robes. Although Ananda had been relieved of the entire two-hundred-and-twenty-seven precepts, Kondanna had requested that he take the first five precepts upon himself, in order that they might protect and accompany him on his journey, and Ananda had gladly consented to this request.

Ananda lived a solitary life in the forest; he ate the fruits, plants, and nuts that he gathered on a daily basis, he slept underneath the shelter of the majestic banyan trees, and spent countless hours meditating on piles of fresh and fragrant kusa grass which he picked every several days.

He was acutely aware of his surroundings, and there was neither sight nor sound that slipped through his consciousness. His consciousness had merged with that of the forest. He had unified it with the birds that serenaded him with their sweet songs and flew from branch to branch. He was at one with the rabbits and squirrels, crickets and grasshoppers, with all of the animals and forms of life that inhabited this forest. He was at one with the soil and the sky, and with the wise trees offering their gentle counsel. Here in the forest, Ananda experienced the interconnectedness of all of life. Every single, minute part of life was entirely dependent on every other single part of life in order that it may exist, and in order that it may live.

Ananda now had a name for the tree whose branches intertwined with his, the fox with whom he scurried across the forest floor, the dove with whom he soared across the open sky, the fish with whom he swam endless oceans, the star with whom he danced under the watchful eye of the heavens, the lover and friend that he so frequently envisioned. He had a name to put with the longing that was stirring in the depths of his being, a name for the beautiful woman who had captured his heart upon sight. That name was Anjali. He knew that he would see her again; of this there was no doubt. He knew this because he knew he would listen to his inner voice. His inner voice would lead him to her once more. The surest way to encounter his soul mate once more was to follow the path that led to his own highest personal happiness and fulfillment.

Ananda rose shortly after daybreak, exiting the forest and walking through a large open pasture. Beyond the pasture were rows upon rows of cultivated fields harvesting rice, flax, millet, and sesame. Beyond the pasture and fields, in the far off distance, Ananda saw a large city. Upon approaching the city, Ananda noticed that it was bordered around the perimeter by a wall made from engraved stone. Several watchtowers stretched into the sky. Ananda continued walking mindfully, until he reached the corrugated iron gates that proclaimed that he was now about to enter the city of Kasi.

The streets were crowded with people flocking from bazaar to bazaar like birds from tree to tree. Ananda walked in the midst of the great commotion when his eyes fell on one of the huts, rather, on what he saw inside the large hut. Sitting ever so serenely and peacefully was a clay statue of the Buddha. Statues of the Buddha were far from uncommon. However, this particular statue instantly brought back vivid memories from Ananda's youth and of the statue in whose presence he had spent many boyhood hours. This statue seemed to be nearly identical to the one from the palace. Perhaps, he conceded, it was a play of his mind, but the shape and texture were profoundly similar. More than the shape and the texture, however, it was the countenance and the demeanour of this Buddha that were the same as the one that he remembered. Ananda had since seen many statues and images of the Buddha. Yet none, up until this very moment, had displayed the same austere countenance that he remembered from the statue he admired during his days as a prince.

The walls were lined with two types of pottery. The first were vessels with strikingly lustrous surfaces, decorated in images of all different colours, from sapphire to saffron, and from deep black to shining silver. The vessels included many dishes, jars, bowls, vases, and earthen lamps. These vessels were round about the surface and symmetrical in shape. The second type of pottery, and it was these pieces that Ananda found particularly intriguing, were the sculptures and statues adorning the workshop. These included those of the Buddha, as well as statues of the

Hindu religious deities, and those of various humans, animals, plants, and other forms of life.

At the rear of the potter's workshop, a burly man was attentively spinning clay on a wheel and shaping it throughout each revolution. The man's jaw was square, his face cleanly shaven and his hair short. He seemed to be relatively advanced in years, perhaps over fifty. Behind the man was a large mud and stone oven that Ananda would later learn was called a kiln. It was used for baking the pottery when finished. The man stopped the work he was doing, smiled, and approached Ananda.

"My name is Surya," the man said in a gruff yet kind voice. "How can I be of service to you?"

Ananda immediately knew this to be the man that had sculpted not only the shapes in this workshop, but also the Buddha statue in the palace that Ananda revered in his youth.

"My name is Ananda. My inner voice has led me into this city and I knew the reason upon arriving at your hut. I felt a surge of energy with which I have long since become familiar. It was at this precise moment that I noticed the Buddha statue sitting in the front of your hut. Upon entering your workshop, I knew immediately that you were the man who was capable of sculpting such a piece as this and unto whom my destiny has called me."

"Well, young man, I am always one to be open and honest, and even diaphanous to a great extent; however, in a strange way I feel highly drawn to you too. I can see that you are well trained in the inner arts, and would assert that you are, perhaps, even a master. You are quite young to be a master but your bearing speaks that this is so. Nonetheless, I am still uncertain as to how I can be of service to you."

Surya had his inklings, yet he wanted to hear the manner in which the young man would articulate his request.

"When I was a boy," Ananda said, "I used to visit a statue of the Buddha and spend hours on end in its presence. Sometimes, I would speak to this statue and it would listen, while at other times we would sit together in meditative silence. This statue has had great meaning to me throughout my life and I am now blessed to have met the man whose head, heart, and hands have crafted this dearest and most beloved statue of my youth."

"How do you know that it was I who had shaped the piece that you so revere?" Surya asked, giving Ananda a curious glance.

"I know that the piece was one of yours," Ananda replied, "just as the mother of a long lost child will, nonetheless, know her child upon their reunion. The statue from my youth is unlike any other that I had seen before or have seen since. That is, until today when I walked into your workshop."

Ananda nodded towards the statue of the Buddha that had first drawn him to the potter's workshop.

"The countenance is the same," he continued, "it is clear that only the most highly skilled craftsman could have created such a piece, as is true with the statue from my youth. Only one who was able to exactly feel the presence and demeanour of the Buddha could sculpt such a work as the one before me now in this workshop and the one from my youth. Furthermore, you bear the mark of a man who is set apart from the rest. It is clear that certain gifts have been bestowed upon you and that you would be capable of creating such work."

"Years ago I was commissioned to sculpt several such statues," Surya replied. "They were spread throughout the homes of high-ranking nobles all the way to the palace. I take it then that, despite your modest appearance, you must be of noble birth and high caste."

Ananda paused. "You are right, reverend sir. Once upon a time I was a prince, but that is of little importance now. I only wish to convey this: the piece that now sits before me possesses that same ethereal quality as the piece I remember from my youth, and I wish to stay on with you and become your disciple. I, too, would like to possess the capability of giving birth to the offspring of my own head, heart, and hands."

"I must admit, once again, that I am drawn to you," he replied. "I am drawn to the mystical presence that you possess. I know not whether this is due to your virtue, integrity, and wisdom, or, perhaps, to some magic spell that you have cast. Do you, however, know anything about pottery?"

"I assure you that I cast no magic spell. I am simply one who is on the journey of awakening," Ananda said. "I know how to listen to my inner voice. It has led me here to you, and though I know nothing about pottery, I do know how to follow my destiny."

Surya gazed ever deeper into the starry eyes of Ananda. The potter thought himself to be dreaming, he viewed his entire life until this moment as if it had been a great dream. He then realized the truth and validity of Ananda's statement as if the life breath of the universe itself had spoken to him.

"Dear stranger, you speak well, and there is an irresistible tone in your voice and look in your eyes. I know that I must provide you with this opportunity. Yet, I know nothing beyond this. If in any way you should displease me, I reserve every right to dismiss you. Your apprenticeship starts tomorrow morning at daybreak."

CHAPTER 8

Ananda rose well before daybreak, his training as a monk had left him with the ability to sleep little each night. Before heading to the potter's hut, he found a large banyan tree beneath which to meditate. Even though he had left the robes behind, Ananda understood the importance of integrating this practice with every endeavour that he pursued in life. When Ananda arrived at Surya's door, the potter was already standing outside, gazing at a full moon that hung in the starlit morning sky. Soundlessly, the master potter motioned for his new apprentice to follow him.

They walked together quietly, each man being a master of silence in his own way, the potter from his long days spent shaping and sculpting, and Ananda from his countless hours immersed in deep meditation. The stillness of the morning, and of the walk they shared, was interrupted only by the occasional song of a bird or chirping of an insect. Surya led Ananda into the forest and then down to the riverbank. The potter reached to the ground and dug some clay with his hands, molding it skillfully.

"This earth, this clay, is the very lifeblood of a potter," Surya said reverently. "In even the tiniest piece of clay there is life, this earth is fully alive. As a potter you must never forget that. The earth itself has consciousness; just as you and I are conscious in our own ways, this clay is conscious in its own way. As potters we must honour the earth and the clay from which we shape our sculptures, statues, and vessels."

"It is clear that you have learned the innermost secrets of the universe through the process of image making," Ananda replied. "The sheer and utter surrender to your craft has given you a form of enlightenment, an enlightenment that surely does not come easily, and an enlightenment that is not in any way inferior to those who devote their lives to the ascetic path. I see clearly that the earth is your teacher, and I wish it to become my teacher as well."

"There are many images inherent in the earth waiting to be brought out," Surya continued, his voice full of gratitude for the earth that was his lifeblood. "It is our job as potters to understand the purpose of the clay that we are shaping. We have to listen to the silent voice within our hearts and it will guide us; this, I imagine is akin to the inner voice that you have mentioned earlier. By doing this, we are able to partake in the creative process, in the shared purpose of creator and creation, for there really is no difference; the creator and the creation are one and the same. It is not up to us to choose through sheer ego or will. Rather, it is our job to become empty vessels and to understand from within. That is the single most important thing you must know about being a potter. There are many potters who do not understand this; still they shape, mold, and create. Some of their work is very good, yet it does not reach the same magnitude of sublimity as the work that comes from the inner sanctum; it is not the same as work that is done through cooperating with the intention of the universe. As creative beings we are here to serve the will of the universe. This is, in fact, our very own will operating at the highest level. We are empty vessels, channels for the energy that permeates throughout all things; our job is to *become* the creative energy."

"You have learned through this process many of the same things that I learned as a monk through meditation," Ananda replied, nodding his agreement. "Through meditation I have realized that I am not only the vessel through which the breath passes, although I am this too, but I am the breath itself. I am the *prana*, the life force, the creative energy. This is my true nature. Many highly realized beings would consider the prana to be something channeling through them but still separate from them; they continue to deal in duality. Until one becomes the prana, then one has not reached enlightenment. You are the second truly enlightened master that I have had the privilege of meeting in my life. The first was Kondanna, the abbot of the monastery where I lived as a monk for six years. Although you have taken diverse paths, you have both reached the same state of realization."

The men returned to the pottery workshop well before the other merchants and craftspeople had arrived for the day's labour. Ananda closely examined the different forms of pottery throughout the workshop, and began to see the potter's devout nature expressed in all of the statues and sculptures there within. It was then that Ananda realized the importance of the path upon which he was embarking.

He lifted his eyes to meet Surya's and then spoke. "I have never been more certain, than in this very moment, that I am meant to be a potter, and that this is to be my form of service and practice. The day will come when I have created my own statues; images that the earth will call me to bring forth from its very being, images that will be called from deep within my being. Through these images that I create, my own realizations of the things I have learned will be conveyed to the observer, and the observer will share in the experience of creation with me. These teachings will be conveyed through the countenance of these figures and through the silent expression that form can create. I am as eager to begin learning my craft as a chick is to hatch from the egg."

"Even the chick has to wait nature's due course," Surya said, laughing merrily. "Over the first several weeks of your training, you will simply observe as I work."

In this period of observation, Ananda resolved to not only take in what he was directly told and shown about the craft but many subtler and more intricate details as well.

"The first thing that we must do is to work the clay with our hands," Surya said, playing with a small piece of raw clay in his mighty right hand. "We do this in order to distribute the moisture evenly and, also, in order to smooth out any air bubbles that may be present in the clay. The texture of a piece of clay is of the utmost importance. It is the texture that best defines the way to shape a piece of clay. In doing this, we must learn to listen to our intuition. The right shape or form will come to us as a feeling; it will feel strikingly different from the other thoughts and ideas that enter our minds.

"Depending on what form we are going to create we will either throw the clay onto the potter's wheel, or begin sculpting it with our hands. If we are making an earthenware vessel, then we throw the clay onto the wheel and begin to turn it. While it is turning on the wheel, we beat it with a paddle to provide it with the round shape that is required of such pieces. For creating the sculptures and statues, and herein lies the real talent of a potter, we must learn how to use our hands. Our hands must channel the creative energy of the universe. They must channel the prana."

Surya began to mold the clay with his hands. Ananda admired his expert touch, at once gentle and firm. The craftsman was strong when strong was needed, and soft when soft was needed. His acute sensitivity to his task amazed Ananda. After several minutes of shaping the clay, Surya held in his hands a miniature lion, whose features seemed to demonstrate the countenance of its creator, at once fierce yet kind. The master potter then handed the lion to Ananda. The potter's disciple was bewildered by the lifelike qualities of the lion that now sat in his hands, and the precision that Surya demonstrated in swiftly yet unhurriedly molding the shape.

"We will allow the sculpture to dry in the sun for several days," Surya said. "When it becomes hard and dry to the touch we will then bake it in the kiln to give its final appearance and texture."

The master potter paused, his eyes straying to the numerous sculptures and statues that lined the walls of the workshop.

"At first, it will take you a long time to mold a sculpture," he said. "I would rather have you take your time and do a good job than to rush and do a mediocre one. The virtue of being patient enough to observe your creation grow little by little, day by day, until it has achieved the sublime readiness that is required of enduring works of the spirit is of the utmost importance when practicing your craft."

CHAPTER 9

The two men sat together on cushions in the dining area of the potter's house. The walls of the large hut were made from stone, mud, and thatched straw. The smell of vegetable curry wafted through the air as a servant was in the kitchen cooking the mid-day meal.

"My daughter shall be home soon," Surya said. "You will be able to meet the pride and joy of my life. There is nothing in this world dearer to my heart than her happiness."

Ananda smiled at the loving devotion of this father. His thoughts fell to his own parents whom he had left long ago in search of the way. He had found the way, his own way, and it had led him to a potter's hut. Had he been right to leave the life of a prince, and then that of a monk? He had vowed to find enlightenment, and to follow the path of his heart, to listen to his inner voice unwaveringly. His inner voice had led him here to a master shaper of images, a servant of sublime works of the spirit, a creative genius. If there was even a fragment of doubt in Ananda's heart about whether or not he was following the right path, it would be appeased by the event that followed.

As the door to the potter's house opened, the name gently floated from Ananda's lips like a leaf falling to the ground on a calm autumn afternoon.

"Anjali,"

"Ananda?"

"Have the two of you met before?" Surya asked incredulously.

"We met while I was still a monk," Ananda replied. "I came upon Anjali while she was doing yoga by the riverbank. She was performing the sun salutations and the morning's oblations."

"I observed this radiant young monk one day when I went to perform my morning yoga routine," Anjali continued. "He was very kind, and when I told him that I had no alms to offer, he asked for my name instead."

As Anjali shifted her focus from her father to Ananda, a radiant smile beamed on her face. "Tell me how it is that you have come to be here, sitting before my father and I?"

Ananda paused, anticipating the multitude of questions that were now swirling incessantly through Anjali's mind.

"I had followed the path of the Buddha to its natural conclusion. The Buddha said that the dharma is like a raft, and it should be used to cross the river. However, only a fool would continue to carry the raft on their back once they have reached the other shore. I had reached the other shore as far as being an ordained monk was concerned and, rather than carry the raft on my back, I disrobed. I was led here by the selfsame inner voice that has lifted me from stage to stage throughout my life, propelling me forwards. Long ago, I was influenced by the statues sculpted by the hands of your father, particularly by one of the Buddha that had been my initial refuge in the dharma. I have now realized that my calling is to form such shapes, to be a potter and sculptor, and to breathe life into the images that lie latent within me. I am now here as Master Surya's disciple and am overjoyed, yet, in some way not surprised, to learn that the daughter that he speaks so fondly of is yourself."

After weeks of observation and cleaning the workshop, the day came when Surya placed a large lump of clay before Ananda.

"Carefully observe this piece of clay with your eyes, your hands, your mind, and with your heart," Surya instructed. "Feel the clay, play with it, knead it, and understand the purpose of this piece of clay. Understand the process of creation that you and the clay will joyously partake in together."

Several days had passed, and all that Ananda had been instructed to do was continue to observe the piece of clay that he had been given. Ananda understood the importance of the task the master had set forth for him.

It was early morning when, shortly after Ananda and Surya had arrived at the workshop, the master potter smiled and asked him: "Do you know what image you will shape through the clay?"

"Yes," Ananda replied, nodding his assent. "Vivid images of Kondanna, the wonderful monk under whose tutelage I learned the sacred teachings of the Buddha, remain imprinted in my memory. In this clay, I can feel that his image will be well represented. I can feel the readiness of his form to spring forth from the clay and be brought to life."

The potter smiled approvingly. "Very well then, your teacher will be represented in this earth. You must realize, Ananda, that to craft a fine piece of work is a lengthy process. It does not happen in one day, it is a process of creation that requires perseverance and patience, steadfastness and stamina. It requires the ability to nurture your creation and watch it grow a little bit each day.

"The growth of a piece of art is much the same as any other form of growth. It happens little by little, day by day. Yet, growth can only be properly observed through larger windows of time. In so nurturing the growth of your creation, you will come to love each piece that you craft with the devotion of a parent loving a child."

Ananda was not in the least bit of doubt that every single piece that the master had ever crafted felt like the very offspring of his head, heart, and hands.

Surya handed Ananda a large palm leaf, a meticulously shaped stick, and a small bowl of dark black dye made from henna powder. He instructed his disciple to draw an outline of the image on the leaf. Vivid memories returned to Ananda as he drew an outline of Kondanna's body. He remembered the way that the venerable monk sat, perfectly still, immersed in meditation. He remembered the round head, soft nose, and smooth brow, the narrow shoulders and thin waist, and the legs wrapped neatly in lotus posture. Ananda finished his initial sketch by drawing the joyous smile and beaming eyes of Kondanna. Ananda realized the extent to which he had really loved the abbot of the forest grove.

Surya, noticing that Ananda had finished, slowly walked over to examine Ananda's drawing. The master potter did not speak a word; his attention was focused on the image on the palm leaf. Through his silence, Surya spoke volumes, and Ananda understood that the master's silent response was, in fact, the greatest praise that he could have paid to his disciple. The surreal, lifelike quality and attention to detail in Ananda's drawing had moved Surya beyond words. If this young man could sculpt half as well as he had drawn this image, then he would become a master, and a member of the guild, in no time.

"This is excellent," Surya finally said, maintaining the poise in his tone. "Now you are ready to use the clay that has been chosen to shape the image of your teacher Kondanna."

Ananda inwardly smiled. He knew deep in his heart that it was only a matter of time before he would master his newly chosen craft.

CHAPTER 10

Anjali had been teaching children to read and write, an altogether uncommon skill, for several years. Ananda admired her for not only teaching these children to read and write, but also for possessing this ability herself; as a prince he had learned and mastered these skills early and had taken them entirely for granted. It was not until he had met many people thereafter who were not in possession of this ability, that he truly appreciated this skill. Ananda not only admired Anjali's intellectual abilities but, even more so, he admired her altruistic nature.

On one particular occasion, Ananda was passing through the village and found Anjali alone sitting contemplatively. Anjali smiled as he sat down next to her.

"You may not realize this," she said, "but my work gives me great pleasure. Much like my father, I am able to see the product of my labour grow a little bit with each passing day. I am able to watch the flowers that I have nurtured blossom and bear fruit. It gives me great pleasure to watch children learn, to watch their expanding minds and hearts at work. It is actually quite selfish of me to teach them, as I receive a sense of satisfaction in knowing that I am able to make a difference in their lives.

"Furthermore, I have come to learn much about life and human nature. Through my work with the schoolchildren I have understood the importance of growth and, most of all, of love. There is nothing more important than spreading unconditional love that asks for nothing in return. Flowers need sunlight to grow, and my heart grieves for all of those children who are not educated, and for those who live in abject poverty. There is nothing that pains my heart more than seeing a young boy or girl without food and clothes.

"Another thing that I have learned through my work with the young is that everything in life is impermanent. Everything that is born must die. I understand the universality of suffering. The first time I really learned this was in a difficult manner with the passing of my mother. At the time I was heartbroken and saddened beyond words, but in some way this mournful event helped me to realize that death is a natural part of life. Death is as natural as birth."

Ananda gazed at her with adulation. "I will tell you a story from the time of the Buddha relating to the universality of death and suffering. There was a woman named Kisa Gotami whom people had thought had gone mad after the death of her son. She went around the towns and villages carrying the body of her dead son and asking various doctors and sages to bring him back to life. One day, a person who observed this phenomenon realized that only the Buddha would know how to handle such a situation. The man sent her to the Buddha. She brought the corpse of her son before the Buddha and threw it at his feet, asking him to bring her son back to life. The Buddha replied that he would help her get the medicine needed for the cure of her son. She would, however, have to perform a certain task. He said that she was to bring back a mustard seed from a home in which no one has ever died. Elated, Kisa Gotami set off on her quest. She went from home to home but she found that someone had died in every home that she visited. By the time she had visited every home in the entire village, she realized that death was, indeed, a natural and unavoidable part of life. She returned to the Buddha, prostrated before him, and asked to be ordained as a bhikkhuni. She later went on to reach enlightenment."

Ananda had intrigued Anjali since they had first met by the riverbank. There was a sense of serenity that he carried on every step of the path, lending to it rare charm. She had yet to see this in another human being. She had seen several other monks and nuns before, but none of them that carried this type of presence. His every movement was careful and precise; he spoke not a single word in vain. His eyes were gentle and understanding. They contained a sense of omniscience about them, as if there was nothing they did not know or understand.

Anjali had begun to learn the teachings of the Buddha, and at times, she, too, had fantasized about the possibility of joining the sangha and becoming a nun. Yet, she knew deep within that she could not do so as her purpose at this time held her fast. In Ananda, she did not see someone who followed the path of the Buddha. She had seen this even from the very first time they had met. Rather, she saw someone who was on a similar quest as the Buddha, someone who was, in fact, a Buddha unto himself. She had resolved to ask Ananda to teach her the way, the way of the Buddha certainly, but more than that the manner in which he had discovered his own way for himself.

Ananda had always been a fast learner and it was with remarkable ease that he began to master his new craft. He had swiftly learned how to shape the clay using the potter's wheel, to use the paddle to smooth and even out the clay, then once the clay had been dried in the sun, how to glaze the earthenware vessels, apply the finishing touches, and fire them in the kiln. He spent his days making earthenware, cleaning up the workshop, fetching clay, and associating with the customers who entered the shop. The new apprentice charmed all of the visitors to the workshop, and they all left with glowing praise for the young man who had now become the disciple of Surya.

It was, however, in the early quiet mornings of each day that Ananda worked on the sculpture of Kondanna. It was in these sacred hours of solitude that Ananda practiced the craft for which he felt the greatest sense of vocation and, also, the greatest affinity. In comparison with making the earthenware vessels, sculpting was a much more arduous task for a potter. This task of sculpting and shaping with the hands required complete focus and unwavering discipline. It was here, however, that a potter could truly express the creative energy freely, and could produce a masterpiece of art.

At first, Ananda began with a very rough outline of the body. He had simply molded the clay into the approximate shape that he would sculpt while leaving plenty of room to spare. He continued for several days, molding only a rough shape. Once he was satisfied with this, his next task was to create the shape of the head. With his hands he fastidiously fashioned the top of the clay mold until he had a round head with which to begin. He then rounded the torso and shaped the legs wrapped in the lotus posture, as Ananda so remembered his venerable teacher.

Once Ananda was certain that he had completed the outline with exact precision, he then proceeded to shape the details that were so well etched in his mind. He began by shaping the hands that rested in Kondanna's lap, right over left, with the palms facing the sky above. He shaped the legs, tapered the arms into the body, rounded the shoulders, and had now completed the entire sculpture except for the details of the face. It was this part that would require the most concentration. The details of the face would either make the sculpture into a living representation of the venerable monk, or would make it simply into that of another man seated in lotus posture.

Ananda began by molding the slightly protuberant ears of Kondanna. Once he had shaped the ears he proceeded to shape the mouth. He remembered the delicate, slightly pursed, lips that were always curled into a smile. After he had finished the mouth, he moved on to shape the quiet and unassuming nose of the monk. Once the nose was complete he shaped the eyebrows, one prominent curved line on top of each eye, and then a scarcely noticeable curved line just above it. Ananda felt compelled to illustrate the master in all his glory, not with his eyes open, but with his eyes closed, in the silent space of meditation. He carefully smoothed over the eyes so that they came out a little bit farther than the rest of the face around it. He brought down the area around the eyes in order that the eyes themselves would stand out. Surya had told him that when forming a sculpture the eyes were always to be left until the end, as they added the final spark to bring the image to life. Even with the eyes closed this was especially true, and upon gazing at his now finished creation, Ananda admired Kondanna as the old monk sat patiently observing the breath.

Ananda realized that even the excitement of finishing this sculpture was ephemeral. It was, indeed, rather short lived and soon gave way to a feeling of emptiness, an emptiness that inherently lay patiently in waiting, even before the project had been undertaken. In some way, once the sculpture was fired and dried it would no longer belong to him, it would belong to the world at large, and to the universe from whence it came. It would no longer be the work of Ananda; rather, it would enter into the myriad world of shapes and images, and become a part of life itself.

Ananda imagined that the feeling he received when this sculpture was finished must be somewhat akin to that of a parent whose child has grown up and left home to enter the world. The allotted task had been completed and with the utmost success nonetheless, but now it was no longer a part of him, no longer his creation. Ananda sat for some time staring intently at the first statue that had been formed from his hands.

As Ananda came closer to the completion of his work, Surya began to give him more time alone in the workshop. The master potter realized the importance of the solitude necessary to produce enduring creations of the spirit. The master understood well that when one is alone and single-mindedly focused on the task at hand, the greatest of creations are capable of being born. Surya, himself having produced timeless works of art, would constantly be leaving for one reason or another. He would leave the workshop for hours at a time, especially in the mornings, in order that Ananda may work in solitude. When the master returned from one such excursion, he found that a pleasant surprise awaited his arrival. The sight of the completed statue brought a radiant smile to the heart of the master potter.

Surya silently arrested himself upon entering the workshop. He gazed first at the statue then at Ananda. Neither man spoke a word. Surya intently studied the piece for several moments before picking it up and examining it with the sight and touch of a master. The vivid beauty of this sculpture was surreal. It had taken Surya many years of practice and hard work before he, himself, had manifested such a work from his own hands. It was only now that Surya realized the extent of the gifts that had been bestowed upon his disciple. Surya quietly rejoiced at Ananda's work and smiled, it was a smile that shines through the eyes.

A full moon glowed in the early evening sky, lending the feeling that it was directly in front of the beholder, and that one could reach out and take it from the sky. This was the day that Anjali had long been awaiting in her heart; the day she would request Ananda to teach her the practice of meditation had come. She understood that meditation was the vehicle to awakening, and the means by which to fully experience the depths of life. She had witnessed monks and nuns immersed in meditation on numerous occasions, and she also saw that Ananda, although he was no longer a monastic, still formally practiced meditation several times daily. She understood that this was the practice that could change her life, lift her life from the realm of the ordinary into the realm of the extraordinary, as it had done for many an enlightened sage since the days of antiquity.

The luminous pair strolled in leisurely silence along the riverbank. They came to a meadow at the edge of a stream leading into the river, and sat beneath a large sal tree that lined the meadow. They looked into each other's eyes. Each saw understanding in the eyes of the other. They experienced that rare feeling that occurs when one looks into the eyes of someone who understands the depths of their being, of someone whom they have known and loved across centuries, many times previously, and for even a glimpse of whom they would traverse epochs.

"I have a request to make," Anjali said. "I would like to ask you to teach me the art of meditation."

"I would be delighted, and out of simple curiosity, for what reason do you wish to learn this sacred art form?"

Anjali gazed at Ananda with reverence. "Perhaps, you do not know this fully and, perhaps, you do," she said. "I shall voice it nonetheless. You have had a profound influence on my life. I have been observing you for some time now and have come to realize that joy is your natural state of being. You are the purest and happiest person that I have encountered in my life. I have observed many people, and all others, without exception, have been subject to various emotional peaks and valleys. However, in you I have noticed something different; your emotions do not control you. There is no tendency to be elated one moment and despondent the next. Anger does not reside in your heart. Neither jealousy nor lust nor greed have you ensnared in their traps. I have noticed these traits in varying degrees in every other human being I have met in my life. There does not even seem to be a single grain of hate that can be found within you. These traits of character that taint the welfare of human beings and cause them great suffering would probably seem so foreign to you that you would not even understand the manner in which their fires consume people. The effects and powers that these emotional constructs can have on people are devastating. I no longer want to be enslaved by my thoughts and emotions. I want to be like you: blissful, joyful, and radiant under any circumstance."

"I have noticed all of these things in you," Anjali continued, "but I have also known that even after leaving the monastic life you faithfully practice meditation every morning and every evening. I have even, on occasion, watched the stillness with which you sit during meditation. At first, the link between your inner peace and your meditation practice occurred to me unconsciously but gradually, after observing you for some time longer, I made the connection consciously. I consciously connected your regular practices of sitting meditation with the levels of serenity, joy, and capacity for love in your heart. Therefore, I wish to learn the art of meditation because I, too, wish to cultivate an inner sanctum in the garden of my own heart, similar to the one you have created for yourself."

Ananda smiled at the sincerity of the beautiful woman before him. On numerous occasions, he had felt her eyes watching him during meditation. He gazed ever deeper into the endless depths of her eyes before continuing.

"I cannot adequately express the joy I feel in hearing the eloquent articulation of your words," he replied. "I will tell you a story about the Buddha that provides the quintessential example of my own purposes for practicing meditation and echoes the sentiment that you have just shared with me.

"A student had once asked the Buddha, 'What is it that you gain through meditation?' The Buddha answered, 'I gain nothing through meditation.' The student was perplexed and asked: 'If you gain nothing, then why do you meditate?' The Buddha, full of boundless compassion, replied, 'It is not what I gain that is important; rather, it is what I lose through meditation that is of the utmost importance. Through meditation I lose fear, anger, hatred, doubt, worry, anxiety, fear of death, and many more things. Through the practice of meditation I lose all of these things and am able to experience my true nature. Therefore, it is not what I gain but what I lose through meditation that is of the greatest significance.'

"This is why meditation is such a necessary vehicle on the path to enlightenment. It is through the consistent practice of meditation that the layers of delusion can be removed. This process is similar to peeling away the layers of an onion. Awakening is a natural byproduct of the removal of these layers of ignorance, and once they have been removed, one is freed from the delusion of samsara and has attained nirvana. Therefore, what is lost through meditation leads us to enlightenment; not what is gained through meditation. Nirvana arrives naturally, of its own accord, when the vessel is empty."

CHAPTER 11

Ananda's fame as a potter spread rapidly. To obtain a sculpture crafted by Ananda's hands was considered nothing less than a great designation of karmic favour. His artwork had propagated widely throughout the land. He had shaped many statues, formed animals and plants, and fashioned the deities. He had formed men and women alike, and had even formed the image of each of his parents.

Ananda had also sculpted several statues of the Buddha as his conscience had dictated to him. The statues of the Awakened One that Ananda had sculpted were certainly his finest works; the deep inward smile and serene countenance of the Buddha shone through in each of these sculptures. It was after seeing the latest and finest of these profound works that Master Surya realized it was time to approach the potters' guild about extending its membership to Ananda as a master potter himself.

In creating the sculpture of the Buddha, Ananda had understood the Buddha's teachings better than he previously had, even better than during his life as a monk. He better understood not only the dharma but also the Buddha's experience of enlightenment. This had become clearer to Ananda than ever before. He understood, once he finished this piece, and even while he was shaping this piece that the austerity of the Awakened One could not be fully transmitted through the teachings or the practice of the dharma. A more visceral approach was necessary; one had to feel the process within themselves by which the Buddha had attained enlightenment. Then, one had to follow the process, however similar or different, that would lead to one's own enlightenment. This could only be done by silencing the mind and listening to the inner voice. Ananda's experience as a potter had led him to the fundamental understanding of the single concept that leads to awakening, the realization of the unity of all things.

Anjali had become a master of meditation. She was able to sit for long periods of time with the fortitude of a mountain. She learned to dwell in the space that exists between thoughts. She learned to observe this space, expand it, and to dwell in it until her every action was performed in complete mindfulness. This regular commitment to the practice of meditation had provided an extra dimension to her life and character. While her life was still devoted to altruism, she was now able to perform the same actions as before with a greater presence of being. The barrier between the external world and her inner world had now dissolved; the two had become reflections of each other, mirror images of the selfsame reality.

Through many a mindful conversation, full of deep listening and loving speech, Ananda and Anjali had come to a point where they understood every grain of the other's being. It was no longer as if they were separate beings, but their consciousnesses truly merged into one entity. The two mystics were perfectly aware of the thoughts and emotions that occurred within the other, and they were also aware of the stillness and peace that occurred in the other.

It was through his devout love for Anjali that Ananda truly began to learn the depth of love that must be extended towards all beings. He loved her with all his heart; yet, he loved her in a way where her happiness rested above all else. There was no possessiveness in his love for her, no sense that she belonged to him in any way. His love for her was sufficient unto itself. He realized that if he could love all beings in the same way he loved Anjali, if he could understand all beings in the same way, if he could feel the same oneness with all beings, then this experience of universal love would be the ultimate experience of enlightenment.

Surya and Ananda casually strolled through light underbrush heading for the riverbank to search for fresh clay. It had been some time since the two of them had gone together to gather clay.

"Ever since the day, several years ago, when you arrived at my hut as a stranger in a white loincloth, I have noticed a dramatic change in everything around me," Surya said, speaking in a nostalgic tone. "There has been a distinct and dramatic change in both my life and that of my daughter. It was as if my whole world was suddenly brought to life; it was as if through your presence, the breath of life had been infused into my world. Your presence brought me alive in a manner that the entire universe has now become conscious of my existence."

"I have also noticed a dramatic change in Anjali's behaviour since your arrival," Surya continued, as Ananda listened intently. "Since the death of her mother, Anjali had devoted her life to the service of others, yet she had borne a solemn countenance while doing so. She rarely displayed happiness, seldom smiled, and had nearly ceased laughing altogether. Her inner turmoil was written all over her features, her grief came through in every expression, transparently visible for all to see, and it had transformed itself into her very demeanour. It was clear to me that she was living a life where every day provided her with a new inner struggle. I had known and felt all of this within the core of my being. Anjali's pain had been my very own; words cannot express how deeply I experienced her suffering. Yet, all of this had changed when you arrived. From the moment she saw you in our house, Anjali was no longer depressed. Her countenance was no longer dismal, and she was instantly as joyous as a songbird. She was the happiest she had been since she was a small child. The long lost gleam in her eyes, genuineness to her smile, and melody to her laugh, had returned. I understood from the first moment that you arrived why my daughter was so happy. Just as I had felt her pain and misery for so long as if it were my own, I now felt her happiness and serenity, as if they too were my very own."

"I am advancing in years," Surya continued. "You are my natural successor, this is no secret. I have approached the guild and they have gladly consented to grant my request. You are now officially a master potter."

Ananda knew that this was the moment he had been awaiting his entire life; for many lifetimes in fact.

"I have grown to love Anjali with all of my heart," he said. "I will always love her. I know that I will love her in joy and sorrow, happiness and suffering. There is no mood, and no season of the heart, that I would not gladly weather with Anjali. With your consent, I would like to approach Anjali for her hand in marriage."

Chapter 12

The consummation of Ananda and Anjali's sacred union resulted in the birth of a beautiful baby girl named Sapna. Sapna was the most wondrous sight that Ananda had ever laid eyes upon. Her fingers and hands, her arms and legs, her waist, her head and face, her curly black hair, ears and mouth, nose and glowing eyes, were all so delicate and fragile, worthy of the ultimate reverence, inexplicably beautiful. Her soft light brown skin was the same as her mother's. The baby had inherited the skin and features of her mother- of this there was no doubt- but the eyes, those eyes that were at once piercing and dreamlike, penetrating and blissful, those eyes she had inherited from her father. The beauty and fragility of new life stood before Ananda in all its glory. He rejoiced at the sight of the delicate flower that was left for them to nurture, in order that it may bloom and bear its sweetest nectar.

In a single glance, the cycle of life presented itself before Ananda. He saw at once the glory of life along with the inherent suffering that is its natural companion. For, even in this baby, even in precious Sapna, the seeds of impermanence had been sown. Her life, too, would come to pass in time; everything that takes birth must also take death. This was the most inevitable premise of life. This child that had just entered the world would one day die, having experienced pleasure and pain, joy and suffering, having experienced love. Under the watchful eyes of the master alchemist of time, this beautiful baby girl would grow up, first into a child, then a young woman, then an adult, into old age, and consequently into death. Then into birth once more, only to follow the same process all over again. This was the nature of the continuous cycle, the nature of the spinning wheel, the nature of samsara.

In his child, Ananda saw the eternal spring of hope and potential. He saw all of those seasons that would return to him no more, and that would now share their warmth and their cold, their clear skies and their rain with Sapna. Ananda pondered the lives of human beings, lives of joy and sorrow, pleasure and pain, of birth and death. As a father, he now saw the ebb and flow of life more clearly than ever; he saw the transience of all things, the rising and falling of the waves in the river of life. Ananda remembered a passage spoken by that great sage of sages, the Buddha. The Buddha had said, "When a person is born into this world, that person is crying while the whole world is smiling; when a person passes on from this world, the whole world is crying while that person is smiling."

Shortly after Sapna's birth, Master Surya fell starkly ill. He found it difficult to arise in the mornings and frequently rested until midday. Nonetheless, he was happy, for, during these mornings spent in bed, although he found it hard to walk and talk, he was often entertained by the company of his newborn granddaughter. He drank the splendour of these precious moments to the dregs, and his thirst was appeased by the wellspring of joy that was Sapna.

On the days when he gathered the strength to join Ananda in the workshop, Master Surya took an exceptionally nostalgic approach to his former abode. He examined every minute detail with a calm, reflective reverence, in the manner of a man who was departing his native soil for the last time. He observed every detail with great attention, seeming to see everything in a different light, as if for the first time. He examined each statue and piece thoroughly, almost all of which were crafted by Ananda's hands now. Although Surya had never told this to anyone, Ananda's work had been far superior to his very own.

Ananda had been the flawless craftsman, skilled and devout, possessing a talent that was only bestowed upon the rarest of individuals. This exalted ability was complemented by an unwavering inner drive, a ceaseless surrender to the exigencies of the soul. Of talent and vocation, it was talent that was the far easier of the two to come across. There had been many individuals with extraordinary gifts bestowed upon them but whose gifts had borne little fruit. To possess that highest degree of talents and have it inextricably woven with a relentless acquiescence to one's calling, were much more exceptional qualities to find in a human being. In Ananda, Surya saw clearly the presence of this peerless blend of talent and vocation.

Surya felt like he was truly observing Ananda for the first time. This handsome man, prince turned monk turned potter, still maintained a boyish charm, the face of a child; he still possessed youthful exuberance and features.

The realization dawned upon Surya fully and deeply that Ananda was a beautiful man. It was no wonder that Anjali had been so attracted to Ananda from the first moment the two had met. Surya released his mind and unfocused his eyes slightly as he gazed at his once disciple.

While watching Ananda he noticed the glow that great sages emit, he saw the brilliant light that enveloped Ananda and he began to see the human energy field. At first, Surya thought this to be an illusion of sorts; he thought his mind and his eyes were playing tricks on him; he slowly came to the realization, however, that what he perceived was entirely real. He remembered as a child long ago he would lie on his back and gaze at the blue sky, when gazing at the sky in this manner he would see tiny flecks of light dancing around. He now realized that even then he was seeing the energy that permeated all things; he had been witnessing the tangible presence of prana. He also remembered gazing at his hands and seeing the presence of the same energy field around his fingers. Yet now, all these things he had once deemed optical illusions, fabrications of the mind, were suddenly all pervading.

Ananda raised his eyes from the wheel where he was turning clay and returned the look of warmth to the man who had patiently and selflessly taught him the craft that they both now shared and mastered. Ananda gently put down his work, walked mindfully to the place where Surya stood, and without a word they hugged each other closely and dearly. Surya left the world smiling, just as the Buddha had said, and died peacefully in his sleep that night.

Chapter 13

Ananda, Anjali, and Sapna meandered through a meadow along the outskirts of the village. Sapna was now three years old. She walked in between her parents, with one of her tiny hands holding the baby finger of each parent. Sapna was an exceptionally gifted child whose ability and determination to learn were startling. Every once in a while, she would release the fingers of her parents, run ahead of them and find some bird or animal to catch her attention. She would then play for a few minutes, falling behind the walking couple, and then catch up again.

Anjali dreamily watched Sapna for a moment. "Children possess a certain magic quality," she said, reverently gathering her thoughts before continuing. "They possess an innocence that, in most cases, fades away all too fast. As people grow up they seem to lose that gleam in their eye, that sense of wonder and curiosity towards life. This sense of wonder, that children possess, is this not the gateway to enlightenment? Do wisdom and enlightenment not begin in a state of awe, in a precious state of innocence that views every moment as being fresh and unique with its own secret to be discovered? Does wisdom not begin in that state where one is genuinely awestruck at the beauty and perfection of life in the present moment?

"As they grow up, all too often, children seem to lose that natural ability to live in the present moment," Anjali continued. "Some children seem to lose it much sooner than others. However, one further thing that I have noticed is that some rare individuals maintain that childlike innocence, that gleam in their eye, or are even able to regain it later in life. Not quite all children lose this ability, and a precious few individuals are able to maintain, or regain, that glorious state of childlike innocence."

The pair exchanged a loving glance, and Ananda doubtlessly understood that his wife was referring to him. He returned his gaze to their daughter, the magnificent young girl whose presence filled him with delight.

"I certainly agree that it is the way in which children observe the world around them that strikes and pleases me the most," he replied, admiring his scampering daughter. "It is the way they observe nature, the clouds, the rising sun, or the chirping birds as if each one of these things is the most extraordinary sight their eyes have ever beheld, and worthy of their total reverence. They observe so keenly, yet innocently.

"While I am often immersed in my own world of thoughts or contemplation, I can observe Sapna and she will bring me back to the present moment by pointing out some interesting detail in our surroundings. There is no squirrel or grasshopper that is not beautiful in her eyes, no bird or insect that does not contain the deepest of life's truths within its very heart, no path or burrow that is not worth exploring. Everything is full of glory in the eyes of this young girl."

The thought could not help but occur in the mind of the master potter that even these days of innocence and purity, these precious days of Sapna's youth, would also pass.

"Sapna will grow up too quickly," Ananda continued, "she will grow up too soon, and in the blink of an eye she will be a woman. The day will come when she, herself, will also be subject to old age, and eventually even to death. The best thing for us to do is to live fully in the present moment, just as children do, enjoying each moment of our time with her and of life itself. The best thing to do is to bask in the splendour that life offers to those whose hearts are open, are filled with wonder, and whose eyes gleam with the innocence of a child."

Ananda would enjoy these days of purity and innocence, and serve every moment of them with the utmost love and devotion. These earliest days of Sapna's youth did indeed pass too soon, as days of purity and innocence always do, and receded into the past.

Years passed and Sapna was now a beautiful young woman. Many men had approached her father about the prospect of marrying this maiden with the soft enchanting brown eyes, and each had been refused in turn. Ananda knew that when the circumstance was right, the flow of life would present the perfect companion for his daughter, similarly to the way in which his marriage to Anjali had occurred. It seemed, moreover, that every man who met the daughter of the master potter fell under her spell. She did not wish it to be so, yet this was the natural power that she had over men. They would simply be enraptured by a single glance of her tremendous aura. Sapna, herself, had little interest in such affairs. She wished to follow the example of her mother; to teach and to help those in need. She had learned to read and write at a young age, mastered Sanskrit grammar, and received the highest education from her mother. She had also observed her mother teaching other children, and the care with which her mother treated all of her pupils. Sapna wished nothing more than to live a life of philanthropic service much like her mother had done.

As much as she wished to emulate her mother, there was an unnamable reverence that Sapna felt for her father. She admired and loved her father beyond words. As a young girl she often stole quietly into the pottery workshop, although Ananda always knew when she had entered, and would sit in a corner of the room to watch her father, serenely focused on the task at hand. Intuitively she realized, long before Ananda had become the most renowned potter in the land that her father was a sage whose path left no trace; the path that he flew left behind an invisible course like the swan rising from the lake and soaring through the open sky. While she wished to follow the path of her mother, Sapna wished to reach the destination that her father had reached. She wished nothing more than to possess that special gleam in the eye, that unshakable inner sanctum whose walls could not be penetrated by external circumstance. She wished to possess that aura of sagacity that bound Ananda firmly.

During the time he was creating, Ananda was seldom seen or heard by anyone. In this solitary manner, his creativity flourished to ever greater heights. He ceased shaping earthenware vessels on the potter's wheel and focused solely on sculpting clay with his hands. It was as if his inner drive only intensified as his fame grew, and he would not find lasting peace until he had shaped all of the images that were borne within him, awaiting expression.

Ananda realized that his fame as an artist was also transient. Indulging in this fame would only be a glorification of his ego; yet, he did not reject fame either, for this too would be a play of the ego. He accepted fame as part of his destiny. Even as his legend grew to improbable heights, he maintained equanimity and held fast to the centre of his being. He also began to see that his name, legacy, and most importantly his work, his creative voice, would continue to live long after he had abandoned the physical body. The statues and sculptures that he had created would stand the test of time. They would be admired by many generations in the future, they would influence posterity. More than any personal legacy, it was the ability to have a lasting voice that mattered to Ananda.

Fame, even long after physical death, still passes; it is impermanent just like anything else. Nonetheless, it gave Ananda a certain feeling of satisfaction that his creative work would continue to live and deal an illusory blow to all that was transient. He knew that it was his calling to shape the myriad forms that had arisen from the depths of his imagination, just as the myriad forms of the manifest world were created from the same life force, the same vital wellspring of prana, of cosmic energy.

Ananda knew well that his work did not belong to him. There was nothing at all that truly belonged to him. He was a wave in the river of life, yet his true nature was that of the river itself. The river would continue to flow;

ever new waves would arise and pass. He was the river itself wholly and undivided. It was the acceptance of his fame that provided the impetus for the final dissolution of his ego.

Shortly thereafter, a familiar man visited Ananda at the potter's workshop. Upon entering the workshop, the man bowed to Ananda with palms together in front of the chest.

Ananda was flooded by memories from his childhood, of a life lived long ago in a luxurious palace seemingly by someone altogether different. His dear friend now stood before him, slightly aged in appearance only. Keshava's eyes, like those of Ananda, had not aged.

Keshava provided Ananda with the news he knew his longtime friend was awaiting.

"Your mother died shortly after giving birth to your brother Mahadev," Keshava said. "Although you did not know it, she was pregnant when you left the palace. Your father has recently passed on the throne to your brother, and your father, himself, has now entered the forest. He was greatly influenced by your pursuit of enlightenment; you have influenced him in a manner that you could never have possibly known. He has now become a recluse and begun his own quest for enlightenment."

Keshava gazed into the penetrating eyes of Ananda. Ananda's eyes had not changed with the course of time.

"The legend of the prince turned monk turned master potter has spread throughout every corner of the land," Keshava continued, "and recently reached the ear of the king of Kosala, your brother Mahadev. He was delighted that the opportunity to meet you was still extant. He sent me here and requests you to arrive with your family to the palace at your earliest convenience."

"Please do tell my brother that we will, indeed, arrive at the palace in several days time," Ananda replied.

A strong yet familiar sense of leave-taking once again overcame Ananda. He had never gone simply to the places where he was needed, for those could have been many; rather, he always went to those places where he was inwardly called. The outer world had always sent its messengers to reflect the inward calling of Ananda's heart. Once again life was calling him, and he knew that he must obey. The time had come for change.

The guiding hand that had led Ananda thus far, that had progressively lifted him from stage to stage throughout his life, was raising its palm once more. The external world had sent its messenger to echo the calling of Ananda's inner voice and bring this calling into manifestation. The external world was simply a mirror of the internal world and the internal a mirror of the external; these two elements of reality reflected one another perfectly, as one went so would the other. The unity of life extended beyond the myriad forms of the outer world, extending to the hearts and minds of all people and beings, both sentient and non-sentient. When his heart had spoken and the timing was right, the universe brought its messenger. Thus, he realized that he was creating the manifest world as he was participating in it. His very thoughts and feelings had an effect on the events that occurred externally, and he knew that it was his perception that mattered most. It was his perception of the inherent unity of all of life that allowed these manifestations to occur.

He realized that as a human being, and active participant in the universe, once he changed his perception then the very objects of his perception began to change in accordance. He was consciously changing the world simply by changing the way that he observed it. By no longer seeing things as separate but, rather, seeing the interconnectedness of all things, then these very things themselves became one. They no longer existed as separate entities; yet, instead they truly became one entity, simply because this was the way in which they were being observed.

As their chariot approached the palace, Ananda was reminded of the days when he, as a boy, would dream of the worlds that existed outside of these very walls. A servant led the company into the front room of the palace. Ananda gazed around the room curiously; he noticed that the room was now populated with many of his own creations in addition to the ones he remembered from his youth. To witness his own work now populating this sacred space of his youth brought him ineffable joy. Next, they were led up the winding stone stairs, past the residence of the noble families and to the chambers of the king. The servant knocked on the door and requested the king's permission to enter with the guests that he had been long awaiting.

"It is an honour and a pleasure to finally make your acquaintance after all these years," the king said. Mahadev had a calm yet commanding presence, the type that is necessary for all great leaders to possess.

"I can plainly see that you have found the enlightenment you sought," Mahadev continued. "I can only begin to imagine the journey you must have traveled and would like to hear more about it soon. I remember well the day when father told me the story of my brother who had followed in the footsteps of the Buddha, and embarked on a quest for enlightenment. Early on, I searched far and wide for you. I went personally to visit several inhabitances of Buddhist monks and nuns. I finally found the one where you had stayed but I had been informed that by then it had been years since you had left. Finally, after I had long given up my search, the legend of a famed potter who had formerly been a monk and, reportedly, was once the prince of Kosala, reached my ear. At first I thought it to be myth, but when I saw with my own two eyes the work that had been created by the hands of this potter I immediately knew this to be the work of an enlightened master. It was then that I knew it was the work of my brother, Ananda.

"I would like for you to resume the throne and take your rightful place as king of Kosala. The people will be highly blessed to have such a virtuous ruler govern the land."

Ananda raised his hand and interrupted his brother before the king could speak further.

"I have no such intentions," Ananda replied. "You are the virtuous ruler that the people of Kosala require. I can see through your bearing that you have the countenance of a king. This is your destiny; it never was mine. My destiny has taken many guises but now it is that of a sculptor, of a creative artist. This is the path that my heart has beckoned me to follow."

"Then, I would like you and your family to stay here with us," Mahadev replied. "We will build a workshop where you can continue to create the finest sculptures in the land."

The king's glance now landed on Anjali.

"There are many opportunities for teaching within our community. You will also have great means at your disposal for other philanthropic acts."

Mahadev's eyes now fell upon the princess in waiting.

"Sapna, you will be able to receive the finest education in the land here in the royal palace, and will be considered nothing less than the princess that you are. I promise that you will not be disappointed with the quality of our instructors, as well as the lifestyle that awaits you."

Ananda looked at both his daughter and wife, and they nodded their approval. "It is with great honour that we accept your offer," he replied, "and I will once again call this palace my home."

CHAPTER 14

The day arrived when a prince from the neighbouring kingdom of Sakya was on a visit to Kosala. Immediately, the young man became irresistibly smitten with the beautiful Sapna. The prince was of noble reputation, and renowned for his courage as well as his compassion. It did not take long for the prince to ask Mahadev, about the identity of Sapna, and the prospect of her hand. Mahadev referred the handsome prince to Ananda, and the master potter immediately took a liking to the sincere young man. Sapna reciprocated the feelings of this prince and was drawn to his kind and dignified bearing. Arrangements and preparations for the wedding were made promptly.

The day of Sapna's marriage was a festive one. The palace was draped in banners of magnificent colours; the entire populace from both kingdoms was in attendance. People splashed red, blue, yellow, green, and orange paints on each other in a celebratory mood; candles were lit throughout in a reverent manner. The nobles paraded on horses, elephants, and camels; the finest musicians and dancers in the land provided entertainment for the festivities.

Ananda and Anjali sat hand in hand on golden thrones. Ananda turned and looked at his ever beautiful wife, gazing into the depths of her eyes, and in that moment he loved her as much as the first day they had met. He loved her laugh, her smile, and her fresh innocence; he loved her strength, her perseverance, and her fearlessness; he loved her devotion, her spirit of service, and her capacity to love all beings. It was in that moment that he fully realized that their time together, too, would pass, just like the waves in the river. He realized that even though they had traveled a long road together, been the worthiest of companions on the journey of life, even though they had married and had a child together, and lived together, slept together, and at times breathed the same breath despite all of this, their journey was each their own. The day would surely come when they, too, parted ways.

Anjali returned the gaze of her husband, staring deeply into the infinite realms of his eyes. She had loved him with every ounce of her being. She also knew that throughout their marriage Ananda had loved her tremendously, but he never had, and never could, have loved her and her alone. Ananda, had in some ways, always remained a monk at heart, and was not capable of attachment. Yet, in not being attached to any one person, the light of his great love for all of humanity was able to shine. She, too, realized that the nature of their relationship was rooted in impermanence, as all things were, and she learned the art of universal love from her husband. He had been her greatest teacher and her best friend; yet, it was these very lessons she had learned from him that allowed her to realize that her journey was her own.

For, as long as they were still together, she might never be able to truly find her own way; she might never be able to tread her own path for herself, for she now yearned to discover the treasures within that her husband had found long ago. Anjali's inner voice was now calling to her, leading her towards new beginnings, and it was a voice she knew she must heed. Without a word, husband and wife, in all the glory of the celebration of their daughter's marriage, poured every ounce of their love into a single kiss.

Shortly after Sapna's wedding, the day came when Anjali approached her husband.

"You have been my companion and my partner on the journey," Anjali said. "You have been my greatest teacher and my best friend. However, it is now time that I venture on my own and find my own way. It is time for me to take the path of renunciation. I know this from listening to my inner voice, that self same inner voice you taught me to listen to long ago, the voice of the heart. It is time for me to renounce worldly life and join the sangha. I have decided to become a Buddhist nun."

Anjali gazed into the loving eyes of her husband; she was, at least in part, making this sacrifice in order that he wouldn't have to. She was making this sacrifice for Ananda, yet she was doing it for herself as much as she was for him. She had realized long ago that this day would come and that it would be much easier for her than for Ananda to take this fateful step. She was now beginning her own spiritual quest; she would live the path of renunciation and practice firsthand the sacred teachings of the Buddha.

CHAPTER 15

"It has all been a dream," Ananda said, noticing Keshava's eyes light up at these words.

"My whole life has been a dream," Ananda continued, "certainly, the events of my life have taken place and all of my experiences have been real; yet, it has all been woven from the same fabric of which dreams are made, the illusory fabric of maya. My life has been a dream, but all throughout I have been conscious of the fact that I was dreaming. Throughout the dream, I have been awake."

"Is this not the ultimate wisdom, to live in the dream and to know that you are dreaming?" Keshava asked. "To live in the midst of samsara and to know, fully and deeply, that you are, indeed, living in the midst of samsara, is this not liberation?"

"Yes, nirvana is nothing more than piercing the veil of maya and liberating oneself from the wheel of samsara through the eradication of delusion," Ananda replied. "Nirvana, then, is a state of being rather than a goal to be obtained. Nirvana is not rising above samsara; it is not rising above and beyond everything that is of this world and of this existence; for nirvana and samsara are themselves fundamentally interdependent; one cannot exist without relation to the other. How can nirvana be a separation from samsara if they are but one and the same thing?

Nirvana can only exist within the framework of samsara, it cannot exist without it; furthermore, samsara can only exist within the framework of nirvana. Maintaining equanimity, the sage dwells in nirvana in the very midst of samsara; the sage is free from the bondage of samsara, free from the delusion that arises when one sees all things as separate. What distinguishes an awakened one from other human beings is the perpetual consciousness that they have of the fundamental unity of life. This realization alone, this state of perpetual consciousness of unity, is freedom from the bondage and delusion of samsara, and is the great liberation, the ultimate enlightenment, the final awakening that is known as nirvana."

"If nirvana is perpetual consciousness of unity, then what happens when the grinding wheel of samsara is brought to a halt? What happens at the very end?" Keshava asked.

Ananda smiled. His smile now resembled that of the Buddha, it was seeking nothing, lacking nothing.

"When it truly ends then you realize that it never began in the first place."

As he replied, time itself had collapsed.

"It is no longer clear to me whether we are old men sitting on the riverbank, or whether we are children," Ananda continued. "Yet, I suppose that both realities are equally true. When I look at you now, I see your myriad forms, I see you as a baby, a child, and an old man all simultaneously. I see you as an ox, a fish, a young girl, and a Buddha. I see all of these forms extant in you in this very moment; your past forms, future forms, and your present form have all merged into one."

Keshava intuitively understood that in this very moment his friend was dwelling in nirvana. In this moment, the final layer of the onion had been peeled. Time no longer existed.

"Once time has collapsed, then the only thing left is love, a love that is purely unconditional and unlimited," Ananda continued, as if picking the questions directly out of Keshava's mind. "This love is the substance from which all things are made. At its most fundamental level, the prana, the life force, is love. Love is the substance from which all of life is born. Love is omniscient and omnipotent. Essentially, the perception of unity is a necessary requisite for love to exist. Without it, true love cannot exist; in order for love to exist there must be a feeling of oneness amongst, and of equanimity towards, all beings and all of life. Then, and only then, can this all pervading love be experienced."

Ananda gazed into his companion's eyes and realized that he was but gazing at his own reflection as he continued.

"When one looks closely at life, this secret is inherent everywhere. It is inherent in the way that a tree bends towards the sun, in the song of a swan echoing in the wind, in a torrential downpour fertilizing the earth. It is inherent in the vapour rising from the sea and back to the clouds again in order that the cycle may continue once more. This secret of interconnectedness permeates throughout all of life, it is the very heart of life itself, and it is this secret knowledge of the unity of all things that rests in the heart of love."

"Love and unity are as inseparable as rise and fall, inhalation and exhalation," Ananda continued. "Where unity exists, there, and only there, is it possible for love to exist, and where love exists there is no more delusion, no more passage of time, and no more treading the wheel of samsara. In that perfect and pristine moment where love exists, and only oneness remains, the deepest secret of life can be felt. The existence of this love is the supreme bliss of nirvana. The journey is in itself the end of the journey."

About the Author

Sameer Grover is an author, poet, teacher, and lover. He was born in Hamilton, Ontario, Canada in 1980. He has studied English, mathematics, and religion at McMaster University, Canada and education at The University of Auckland, New Zealand. *The Prince and the Potter* is his first novel.

Visit Sameer at **www.sameergrover.com**